A *not so* NORMAL FAMILY

A NOVEL

RON IANNONE

Destination Press
Morgantown, West Virginia

ISBN: 978-09982020-3-7

DEDICATION

In memory of my mother and father.

Everything is deepening gloom,
A foreboding of my very doom.
—Bernard Shaw

Bo-Jean

I'm dead. But in a place that I can tell my story. Here, it's semidark and cozy warm. There is soft white light everywhere and I feel each day I'm floating around going nowhere, looking down on the other world I came from. Down there they say when I die I'll meet all my close relatives, my mother, my father, my uncles, my aunts . . . . I see them when I think about them as they were when I was young and they were in their thirties. The other day I saw my dad. He had on one of his favorite red bow ties on. We spoke about nothing in particular but just understood it was good being with each other again and perhaps one day soon he will take me horseback riding on one of the racehorses he owned. I always loved those times we rode together. I've never been so relaxed in my life here. It's like I've taken a whole bunch of Ativans without the hangover feeling afterwards. I don't know how I got it, but I have a solidly built oak desk to write on while sitting on a soft blue cushioned, comfortable chair. My name is Bo-Jean and how I got it is not clear except my mom liked the name because of a country singer named Bo-Jean Rider. I'll get to my mother later on. I think it's important to let you know that I have a master's in English literature from Yale. I always wanted to be a writer since the time Miss Green grabbed my little notebook I was writing in and she read it aloud to the class. It was about how much I loved Billy Malone, especially his beautiful black curls that staggered here and there on his sexy-looking neck. And that's how Miss Green read it. My face became beet red and hot with embarrassment. My classmates laughed as she read about my feelings for

Billy. However, a few students did laugh nervously and I know felt sorry for me.

Later on I had a career in New York City working in PR for the designer Liz Russ. I also met and became great friends with Kay Fanning. Besides this, I met and fell in love with a cop named Larry Myers. Tall, dark, handsome and wonderfully built. We got married soon after we dated for only a few months, and I got pregnant. Right now, I can't remember the act of intercourse that produced my daughter Roberta. Larry accepted a position as police chief in my hometown of Port Byron, New York. I liked the idea of going back home. I was getting tired and bored with the single scene in New York, even though I knew I would miss Kay. I also knew I would have to deal with the one incident that happened to me when I was twelve. Larry and I also had another daughter named Stella who was born twenty-four months after Roberta was born. Then our marriage went to shits because I became bored with being a wife and mother. I began to go out and drink heavily, looking for some excitement. Larry caught me in a motel with a guy named Clarence whom I later married but soon divorced because he was seldom home.

Stella is sixteen now and has Asperger's. Roberta is eighteen and seems to have some identity issues. We are in therapy with a therapist named Jeanie Castro. She's nice, but I don't know if she's helping me. I don't know about the girls. They tell me after they see her, or we see her as a family, they feel better. But, I seem to be stuck and have been stuck for years and year after year I can't get out of this stuckness.

It has been twenty-eight years since what happened in the bowels of my elementary school, I have tried hard not to think about it, but I do all the time. Now and then I looked in the mirror and saw that I had a small, bird-like cutesy face. I always thought the best part of me was a well-shaped ass. Breasts were small, but the guys all liked touching my ass. I used to dream that the huge scar on my arm was black.

One of the first courses I took at Yale was from Professor Shaw, Scott Shaw. He was short and very thin, with curly, grayish-black hair. He had these beautiful haunting brown eyes. He was a poet and novelist who was published by the University Press.

Along with me, all the girls loved him. He was so smart and witty.

"If you people don't plan to write, write, and write, then leave class now," he said in a very serious manner. He went on: "I want all of you to dig deeply into your voice and better understand who you are and what life means for you. Of course, if you don't do the work, this class is probably not for you. Is that clear?"

Most of the students nodded their heads yes. I thought to myself, *I will do anything for you, Professor Shaw.*

For the first assignment, he wanted us to write in the first person about one happy and also one sad experience in life. He didn't want us to use a lot of flowery language. For him, clarity meant making simple, distinct, and powerful sentences. "Say it and get out," he said strongly. I saw that he was married as he pushed his hair back. The silver ring I quickly noticed shining brightly.

I wrote a description of going horseback riding with my father, Fred. He died when I was fifteen. He loved spending time with me on Saturday afternoons. He rode an older horse called Steely, and I rode a younger sleek beautiful black horse called Mister Clean. Their names were selected by the trainer who helped my dad race the horses around the track. As I was riding Mister Clean one day, he stumbled over a large rock. He broke his leg and had to be put to death. I cried for days after thinking I was a curse for my dad's horse. My dad showed me it wasn't my fault, and I should not carry such a burden. The very next day he had me on another beautiful black horse called Julie. Everything went fine riding, and I loved my father even more because he brought me back to loving horses again.

Professor Shaw looked at our papers, and then he gave them to us to look at. At the end of class we had to give them back.

Fine job. Splendid description of your love of horses and your father.

"I really liked what you wrote, Bo-Jean," he said as I was walking out.

I felt happy that he was pleased, but I also was confused about my feelings for him.

"Bo-Jean, you don't sound like a country girl. You sound smart."

I didn't know what he meant. I knew my paper was okay, and I knew others in class had better papers, especially June and Stanley who were very bright. He sometimes made fun of them when he read their papers. They had talent whereas I thought I was just competent. When reading their papers out loud, he made them sound phony, and when he read my paper, he made it sound like it was the best.

The class got another assignment where we had to keep it under one page. He repeated, "Say it and get out. That's the key," he said.

An Unexpected Experience
By Bo-Jean Franklin

I decided to walk to the theatre on Broadway. *Where do I go now?* I thought. Because I knew that I still loved him even though he was dead. It was a spiritual love I now had for Peter. The afternoon sky was dark and dreary and it looked like rain. The blowing of the horns and thud of tires going over manhole covers matched the excitement I felt for Peter. Rapid-moving streams of people flanked both sides of the clogged Broadway Avenue. I opened the doors to the theatre and said hi to the box office staff. I felt an exciting shiver move through me. Just then Peter whispered in my ear, "Think about me all day."

"I will."

"Good," he said.

There he was, now in front of me. He looked great as he did twenty years ago. He had on tight fitting jeans and a black turtleneck. His lips were wider and his eyes were bright as ever. His black hair was long and pulled back in a ponytail.

I smiled, and he smiled back.

Dear Bo-Jean. This is coherent and well ordered. It's like poetry. The country girl can write beautifully. Let's talk about your future. I feel your soul. SS

Why was he centering on me? I didn't see other students getting comments on their papers like me. He seemed truly interested and kind to me. This made me feel good. It just worried me that he may lose interest in me and center on Audrey who had beautiful, long blonde hair and was super bright. I knew some of the other students were hanging out with her because they were hoping for getting the same attention. I wondered when we would get together. I had been to his office only once to pick up some of my papers. It was a large office with high ceilings and tall windows. The furniture looked soft, especially a dark leather sofa he had in a small alcove with wall to wall bookshelves. Usually a bunch of us would walk with him to his office as he talked about the beauty of language and how good writing is like a great piece of musical composition. This one time it was just him and me walking. I was terribly nervous but excited about our being together.

"Did anyone tell you you have mysterious deep blue eyes?" he asked me.

"No," I said, blushing.

"Well, you do," he said, smiling. "Those eyes and your mature insights are very attractive to me."

I didn't say anything, hoping he would invite me in to his office. He did.

He told me to sit down as he took a call. I believed it was his wife because he was telling her he would pick up some groceries, but the more he talked the more agitated he became, and his mood became dark. I noticed his desk was disorganized with papers piled here and there. He hung up and seemed pissed off as he looked at his papers on his desk.

"How would you like to be my student assistant?" he asked. "It's not much money, but you can learn a lot from reading other papers. I think you're at a point where you can help me grade papers, answer phones, and do stuff like that. I have too many papers and classes. At Yale, they take advantage of junior faculty. Anyway, do you want to help me?"

"Sure," I said, holding back my excitement.

"Good," he said. "You know I don't normally use student assistants, but there is something about you. I don't know; maybe it's your vulnerability, your true self is hidden away. I think I would like to get to know that."

My head was swimming with joy. I didn't say anything as I looked at a picture of his wife and two kids sitting on his desk. She was beautiful with long sandy brown hair and big blue eyes. She looked like the actress Julianne Moore.

"Look, can you come in tomorrow at four and I'll get you started?"

"Okay." I stood up as he came over to me and softly touched my arm. Everything was turning inside of me. I couldn't wait to come back tomorrow.

I spent the next day thinking about him and daydreaming

about his coming over to my room in the dorm and asking if I wanted to go to dinner because his wife left him.

The next day I went to his office, but he never showed up. I hated him. Typical male. They get you all hot and bothered and then drop you.

The next day in class I refused to look at him. Asshole. At the end of class, he said, "Bo-Jean, will you stay for a moment?"

"Look, Bo-Jean," he said. "I'm sorry, but something came up at home. My wife is a also teacher here, and something came up and I had to pick up the kids."

"I understand," I said. I thought how I got all dressed up for him yesterday. I was still angry.

"I see you're really upset. Again, I'm sorry. Let's go to my office. I'm so behind."

"Okay," I was feeling much better. I wanted to show him that I knew my stuff about grammar. Right now I wanted to be with him all the time.

When we got to his office, he threw his briefcase and papers on his desk. Then he led me over to the sofa. Gently, he turned me around and kissed me. Then before I knew what was happening we were lying on the sofa. I loved his touch and the feel of his skin. Everything about that other time with Jimmy stayed buried in the dark part of my mind. I knew I loved him now and always had. With him, I could do everything I thought was morally wrong. His wife would divorce him because of his love for me and I would marry him.

Sometimes I would correct papers and he was very businesslike. I knew nothing was going to happen. We didn't do it very often, but when we did, he was so tender. Sometimes those other thoughts about that bad time popped in but his tenderness made them go away. This time I truly felt I was losing my virginity. There was blood, but it was only a little. The other time it came gushing out.

He left for vacation, and I didn't know what I would do. I told him I would come with him and be his nanny or maid. Of course he said that wouldn't work. And for the next two years the relationship went on, and I told him about everything. I told him how much I loved my father and how I still couldn't get over his death. My love for horses. Also I told him about my grandmother and grandfather. They would take care of me when my mother and father would go to work. My mother was a top executive in a shoe factory until it closed and moved south. That happened in my senior year of high school.

There was something wrong with him when he came back from his vacation. He seemed cold and distant. We made love, but it seemed perfunctory and more hurried. Nothing seemed right. Many nights I would cry myself to sleep, knowing that the end was coming. And it did.

In December of my last year, he walked in as I was correcting papers and said, "Bo-Jean, I can no longer be intimate with you." He was now standing over me as I sat on the couch. "My wife is leaving me because she found out about us and others I've had relationships with. I'm sorry. It's been fun. I care for you, but I need to get my life together. I'm leaving Yale in January. I have accepted a job out West." He leaned over and kissed the top of my head like a father saying good-bye to his daughter.

Angrily, I got up and threw the papers on the floor.

Crying uncontrollably, "Is that it? For almost two years I've been your slave in work and sex. I hate you." I shoved him hard, and he fell against the desk. I left, slamming the door behind me, and headed nowhere. Later, I bought two gallons of red wine and went back to the dorm and drank and drank. I thought of jumping out the window but was too drunk and tired.

I woke up Monday morning with the same clothes I had on

when I left Scott's office. I smelled like shit. I hadn't eaten and wasn't hungry. There were several voicemails on my phone. I didn't care. I needed to take a bath. There was a bad taste in my mouth from the wine.

Later that day I answered the phone. It was my friend Mary.

"How come you weren't in Shaw's class today?"

"I am dropping the class."

"Why?"

"He's a bore and an asshole."

"I thought you liked him and worked for him."

"Not anymore. I need to be free and get on with my life."

"Can I help?"

"No. I'm fine. I really am. I'll see you tomorrow sometime."

"Okay."

I still thought Shaw loved me and wanted me to chase him, probably like others. I didn't want to be one of his love things. I knew he was going to miss me and the sex I gave him. So what, I hated him. I now had another wound that could not completely heal.

My mother, Anna, who now lives with us, has begun showing signs of Alzheimer's. Yesterday she asked me if I was always fat. I'm overweight by ten pounds but not really fat. Yes, I've been wanting to do something about my belly and hips.

I remember I loved when my mother had to leave for work early. She would pick me up from my bed and place me in the bed with my grandmother Louise and grandfather Pat. Their bed was always so warm and cozy. They would cuddle me up in their arms and hold me close to them. Sometimes my grandmother would get up and bake homemade rolls. Then she would come back to bed and wait until they were cooked. The fresh smell of bread baking, their warm bodies against me, and the spilling of sunlight through the sheer curtains made everything seem perfect to me.

Some days I wish I wasn't married and could be in New York City again with my friend Kay whom I see every few weeks. She works now as the VP for marketing at Russ' House of Fashion. She is single, tall, and beautiful. She is everything that I want to be but can't because of willpower.

My cell phone rings as I am picking up the house.

"Hello," I say.

"Mrs. Franklin?" someone says in a sweet fake voice on the other end.

"What can I do for you?" I hate to be bothered when the house seems to be a mess.

"Mister Silverstein would like to see you around two today."

"Why?" *I just want to get everything picked up—socks, T-shirts, baseball hats, blouses, and so on.*

"Stella has been having some problems."

"What kind of problems?"

"He'll talk to you about that."

"Okay, I'll be there."

In my mind, I think Stella's Asperger's is not bad. Every day she dresses up in cheap dresses we buy from Walmart. I wish my other daughter, Roberta, would be more conscious of dressing like a girl. Stella likes to look pretty. Even though everything hangs on her because she weighs about ninety pounds. Mostly, she eats Fruit Loops but with only the blue loops. Sometimes I think my daughter is from outer space. She just stares with her huge, brown eyes when I talk to her and other times doesn't seem to answer when people talk to her. She seems to be in a strange place talking to aliens. She never dates boys, just likes to look dressed up for school. Her beautiful, long, sandy blonde hair reaches down to the middle of her back. She does well in her subjects, not great but okay. She seems to be daydreaming all of the time.

Sometimes I yell, "Stella, snap out of it."

"What?" she asks.

"What are you thinking about?"

"Nothing," she says in a dazed and far-off world voice.

Where does she go? I wondered. I think she seems locked in her world and is just passing through this world until she passes to the other side.

Stella has an uncanny ability to tell me every piece of clothing she has in her closet along with each pair of shoes she has. Also, you never know: she will be going for days with nothing happening until she bursts forth with a tantrum because of a loud noise or a light flickering or someone touching her. Any of these could send her off for hours. I don't know how Asperger's exactly works. I just know Stella will be standing with you and then, boom, you turn around and she's gone.

Once in a grocery store, my shy beautiful girl went ballistic because of the freaking sound of the fluorescent lights. It was like she was having an epileptic fit as she bounced from one shelf of groceries to another until I held her so tight that she went limp in my arms. Of course, shoppers, workers, the management—all came running.

I said, "She's having an episode. Stop looking. She's not a monster. Just give me a second. Don't worry. She won't hurt you." I say that and sometimes I just don't know about her, especially since I've bought two pistols so we could go together and target practice. It seemed to be a good idea at the time. Sometimes I worry that when I bring a guy into the house I'll have to protect myself, and I think Stella should be able to protect herself too. She seems to love the idea of buying those pistols and shooting together. Even though I'm no longer married to Larry. Being a cop, he thinks it's a good idea for me to have a gun around to protect myself. Also, he knows I roam around at night and worries that something bad will happen to me, whereas Clarence wasn't around long enough to care one way or another. On the other hand, I never take a gun when I go to bars.

STELLA

She's yelling again from downstairs to hurry up or we're going to be late for school. I don't fucking care about school. Soon there will be no school for me and a lot of other people. However, I like the same schedule every morning: get up at 6:16, shower at 6:18, get dressed at 6:30 in a new dress. They must be different every day. I know they look cheap and sometimes too big for me. But I like looking like a model I see in fashion magazines. I put on very little makeup, just enough to darken my blue eyes and some flesh makeup to make me look alive—because my skin is so pale. I heard a comment behind my back one day that I looked like a vampire. Yesterday's anonymous text to me was: *Why don't you drink some of your sister's blood you stupid fuck face.* The dress is always below the knees because my mother said I shouldn't look like a whore who wants it. At around 6:50 I take the Adderall so I can concentrate somewhat and don't go wild like yesterday at the grocery store where I pushed all of the Hunts tomato sauce cans off the shelves. Order was back when I came home and buried myself under the thick comforter on my bed, along with all the cozy brown Teddy bears.

I also know that Mister Silverstein will be calling about the incident in the library where Anthony Bucca called me a fucktard and I lost it and started tossing classic books like *Moby Dick* and *Pride and Prejudice* at his ugly head. I think I also bit his ear.

"Okay, Okay, I'm coming!" I yell, as I go downstairs so she'll stop fucking yelling for me to come down. Before I leave my room I make sure in my bathroom I fold my blue-colored washcloth and its matching towel into perfect squares. Both are hanging on the towel rack, with the washcloth to the left.

On the way down I also check the small, corner pocket of my light blue backpack to make sure my light blue rosary beads are in there along with a perfectly folded, frilly, beaded, black handkerchief on top. I am forgetting to mention that before I leave my room I check my closet; I open the large black gun case that holds a TEC-DC-9M pistol and a 9 mm Hi-Point 995 carbine. I rub them both for luck before I leave. I can't believe my mother doesn't care that I have guns in the house. She thinks I'm protecting her. She's becoming a pretty good shot like me. However, she doesn't know about the other stuff. Tonight, I think, I need to sneak out again when she's asleep to see that stuff in the storage unit. I love wearing my black hoodie and sweats when I go. I blend in nicely with the evil of the night.

Once downstairs I grab a bowl of my Fruit Loops, taking every color out except for the little blue pieces. Then, before I go out the door, I wipe the doorknob with a Kleenex. My mom follows. She works two days at home and the other three for Gold Printing. I know she would rather be working for a big publishing firm in New York City. Having a master's in literature in Port Byron, New York, is no big deal.

When I see my father, Larry, this weekend, I want him to know that Mom is going out a lot at night. I wonder if he really left because of me and my episodes. For twelve years, I loved having him around, even though his police job took him away. When I ask my mom why they broke up, she says it wasn't a good fit. "You mean like a shoe," I remember asking her. She got mad and just said, "Stella, stop being such a wiseass."

My father is the police chief and a police investigator with the Port Byron Police Department and is now married to a former meter maid. All boobs but no brains, they say. Every other weekend Roberta and I go over to their house. For the most part, our dad takes us to the movies, malls, concerts, and museums in Syracuse, or sometimes he takes us to New York City to visit his parents and see a Broadway play. Irene, his wife, never comes. She tries hard with us, but I think I scare her because of my condition. Last weekend we went to see the musical *Next to Normal*. I loved it. The dad's an architect. The mom rushes around to pack lunches and pour cereal; their daughter and son are bright, wisecracking teens. And yet their lives are anything but normal because the mother has been battling manic depression for years. The whole thing is about mental illness, and it hit home thinking about me, Roberta, and my mother.

"Bye," she says. "I'll be here at 2:45 to pick you up. I have to see Silverstein earlier. You know what that's about?"

"No," I said.

Another anonymous text: *Why don't you kill yourself, fag* . . . .

Port Byron Mainland School is full of assholes. All the students think I am a freak and a weirdo. I once tried to go on a date in my freshman year. It was disastrous. He tried to kiss me, but I kicked him hard in the balls.

As I walk toward the school, I hope tonight on TV it's about a serial killer. I love reading about them and seeing movies about them. I can always use more material for my little black notebook.

Gary Leon Ridgway—Green River Killer; American. Convicted of 48 murders, then confessed to almost twice that. Typical victim: prostitute or other vulnerable woman/girl; strangle them and dump bodies, sometimes coming back to fuck them.

1969, age 20: graduates High School, marries 19-year-old girlfriend Claudia Kraig. Joins Navy, sent to Vietnam: on supply ship, saw combat. In military, starts screwing lots of prostitutes. Gets gonorrhea, keeps going—unprotected, of course.

Friends & family described him as "friendly but strange." (Isn't every murderer/rapist/etc. "friendly but strange" or "seems nice but keeps to himself"?) First 2 marriages—divorces because they were all sleeping around. Got religious during the second marriage. Tried to convert door-to-door, read Bible aloud at work and home, forced wife to subject herself to strict pastor.

All his women—wives and girlfriends—said he couldn't get enough. Demanded they all fuck several times a day. (Obvious) speculation about him being torn between uncontrollable lust and strict religious beliefs.

ROBERTA

I walk downtown and turn left on Division Street. It has a Hot Spot. Being eighteen, I'm old enough to go in. Port Byron has over 1,300 people, and probably since the state approved these places, we have a total of two Hot Spots in the village. I started going to this one about a few months ago. Usually I walk in with sunglasses and my fake beard I used in a play I did in Mr. Curtis's class, the only class I feel free in. Sometimes I'm asked for my ID, but now nobody bothers me. I play slots but basically I watch the other people here. My ID says "Roberta," and even though I have a beard, nobody in here questions me because they want the money. When someone asks me my name, I tell them it is Robert.

Ever since I was about five I knew I wanted to be a boy. I never really liked dolls and frilly stuff, but I couldn't tell my mother because she was dealing with Stella and her problems of Asperger's. Sometimes I hate Stella because of all of the attention she gets. Sometimes I want to beat her head in with all her dresses and matching shoes. Of course, my father doesn't know. Macho cops have problems with transgender people and even gays, even though they pretend to accept them. I just don't know how he would feel. He seems open to diversity and an open society. He has five cops working for him. Three are black and one I believe is gay. Someday I need to talk about it with him and what's going on in my life.

Anonymous text: *So what's actually down below? Pussy or dick?*

In short, I love coming into these Hot Spots because most of the people are old and retired. I think most of the people here blow their social security checks or pension monies. I spend the money I steal from my mom's purse. She gets an alimony check and a little bit from the printing company she works for. Here, I feel safe like I was in church.

I try to understand Stella, but I can't understand what sends her off—like lights, loud sounds, touching, or even someone touching one of her dresses. One time she almost broke my arm because of that. Even though she looks pale and weak, she has the strength of a muscled hulk. I don't know how much longer I can keep hiding because I'm having feelings for a boy, especially in my English class. He's tall, thin, and has beautiful blue eyes. I get all goofy when he talks to me. I think he wants to date me as a girl. I don't know sometimes who I am—a boy or girl—because as Robert, I like girls. The bartender here is about twenty-two and female. I have wonderful sexy dreams about her when I'm in the shower.

Today I have won about twenty-five dollars, but most of the time, as I said, I just observe the other patrons and listen to what they talk about. Usually they talk about local politicians whom I never heard of. I never read the papers. I like Facebook, Snapchat, and text a lot with my friend Pam. Pam has gone with me to the He/She Nightclub for the drag show. A lot of the seniors in my class say they have gone. I go because I like to dress up as a guy and entertain people by doing karaoke songs, especially by Frank Sinatra. They love my "Fly Me to the Moon."

Anonymous text: *You Butch asshole, kill yourself before we do.*

Larry

Bo-Jean hasn't called me in two days, and that is good. I don't know what she wants to do when Stella grows up. It is what it is. She gets a lot of money from my alimony, and, thank God, Irene is still working and has been promoted to assistant parking director. I'm working on the Sandy Brown overdose case and her death. I remember her coming to one of Stella's birthday parties. That was when Bo-Jean was trying to integrate her into so-called normal teenager activities, but it didn't work out because she hid under the dining room table, covered up, in a fetal position screaming, "I hate parties, I hate parties."

Anyway, I remember Sandy, a petite young girl with short blonde hair.

Her mother calls every day, wanting to know how she got the drugs.

"Mrs. Brown, we aren't sure yet. We think she got the drugs in school."

"Do you know who it was?"

"No, I don't."

"All her friends seem so nice. They don't seem like kids who would do that."

"I understand, Mrs. Brown. Give us some time."

"I don't have much time, Sir. I've been dealing with breast cancer."

"Sorry. Look, we have found out she was dating a guy who we know was dealing in drugs."

It seems she and this guy had a strong relationship. The coroner found a fetus three months old in her. There was no way I could tell Mrs. Brown that her daughter was three months pregnant and had been in a serious relationship with a black guy who was a drug dealer.

Bo-Jean

Last night, I know, at some guy's party I talked and talked and drank and drank until I think I fell over a sofa. I remember some bald-headed guy bringing me home and trying to have intercourse with me in his car as we parked in front of my house. I really didn't feel anything as I thought about Stella—when she opens and closes her bedroom door over hundreds of times. Just like when she played with her dolls: she would play with a doll without a head for several hours. I think now that the guy thought I was aroused as he licked my ears as he penetrated, but my mind was still on Stella. Also I think maybe it was last year I got so depressed I tried sticking my head in the oven. Suicide sometimes seems to me to be a relief from the misery of the world. I pushed him away, quickly opened the car door and ran to my house.

I seemed so stressed out all the time now, like I feel I'm going to blow up inside. I need to calm down. Then there are days when I get up and write poetry. "I love early mornings . . . when you can see the sunrays coming down through the trees . . . The birds are singing . . . The air is clear . . . The trees seem to reach to the sky for their strength . . . listening to the whispers of the universe that is carried on a breeze . . . Or to the songbirds that hang on their branches to sing . . . While deeply rooted they are there . . . to provide protection, to provide a home, to provide shade and fresh oxygen for all living things . . . ." I should write more and also paint. It brings some peace to my troubled soul. I need help.

Stella

Before I open the doors to the school, I take out my handkerchief and wipe down the huge, brass curved doorknob. Quickly, with my head down, I go to my locker and pulled out what I need for English composition and advanced college math. I place them in my backpack and hurry toward my math class. I look inside the window of the door and see almost everyone in there. Angelina, an overweight girl, pushes ahead of me and opens the door, and I follow. Thank God, I think, I won't have to wipe the doorknob down. I head to the back and take a seat. Everyone looks at me as I sit. Mr. Walters is a fat-cheeked teacher, sloppily dressed in a red-checkered flannel shirt with wrinkled khaki pants. He is talking about binomials and factoring. I know this stuff. I hate it when we repeat stuff we've gone over and over in previous math classes. I see Alice looking at me now. I would like to get to know her. She's a skinny redhead with a warm smile. Every day she tries to talk to me, but I put my head down. However, yesterday she asked me if I like the band Maroon 5. I said yes and talked to her until the bell rang, and we both went to our next class. No one else will talk to me because I'm the funny-looking girl with autism or, more specifically, Asperger's. I wonder what they would think if they knew I was into school killings and love reading about serial killers. Recently, I read about Aileen Wuornos, one of America's most famous female serial killers. She said, "I robbed them and I killed them, and I would do it again, and I know I would kill another person because I've hated humans for a long time."

Also, as I read about Adam Lazaro killing all those little kids in Connecticut. I see myself like a female Adam Lazaro but would never kill little kids. I just hate it when I go to my locker and they snicker as I pass them. Also I can't help but laugh my ass off when I see videos of the shit-faced, cross-eyed guy with light red hair who killed all those people in that Colorado theatre. Lately, the jihad killings in Paris and California interest me. The school counselor, Mr. Smithfield, says I should develop interests like so many girls now who are into sports. I don't think the girl jocks would like that because they have their special clique, and I know they would think an unathletic sluggish person like me would hurt their image. Some of the girls may like my hair. Perhaps the world thinks I might be good looking and should belong with cheerleaders and not with athletic types. My mother says I've got to make more friends. She wants to invite kids my age over, and I tell her if she does I will hide like before. I know she doesn't understand why I like shooting the pistols so much, but she says it's okay they are in the house with her, being a single woman and all of that. Thank God, she doesn't know about the storage unit, having all those guns and stuff for pipe bombs. The guns I got from mail order but the others came from the streets. It costs me sixty-five dollars a month to rent the unit, and little by little I take it from her purse. I think Roberta also takes money from her. I now understand why my mother is broke most of the time.

Anonymous text: *We just want Americans in this school not freaks who can't talk. Leave now!*

Bo-Jean

One morning a couple weeks ago I had something happen that has been happening every so often, I woke up on the kitchen floor covered in blood. My head ached and my nose was bleeding profusely. I was scared. The last thing I remember was that I came home from the bar Curley's alone and as I sat down everything went fuzzy.

I decided I would walk to the ER. I was only ten minutes away. The doctor checked me and said sometimes these blackouts could be fatal. And so on. He said drink more water. That night I went out and got a gallon of cheap red wine.

LARRY

I know Bo-Jean thinks I don't care for Stella or Roberta, even though I see them every other weekend. Very often I drive by the school when Bo-Jean is dropping off Stella. Other times I see Roberta when she walks home. Then she seems to vanish. Sure, we were both having affairs when we were married. I think now these guys help her with her loneliness, and most important, dealing with Stella. I also hate that she still calls me about creepy guys hanging out at the Casey Park playground. Last week she called about a Post Office truck parked on the street. We checked, and he was only sorting out packages.

I am really up to my head in the overdoses that are happening in central New York. It kills me when we have to tell the parents their daughter or son of seventeen is dead. They go into shock and stunned horror anyway. I wish Bo-Jean and Irene could be friends. But Irene hates Bo-Jean and vice versa. I don't know what Bo-Jean wants out of life. She wasn't a big believer in women's libber stuff. Yet, when she got mad, she was full of female aggression. I felt, when she got so mad at me, she could pick up a knife from the kitchen counter and stab me a hundred times with pleasure. Bo-Jean had this dark side to her, which she shared very little of with me. One night, she did tell me something happened to her in elementary school and that's why she had a scar on her arm. Jimmy Watkins, she said, is in jail because of what he did to her. She never really wanted to talk about it. She was good at burying things.

Bo-Jean

No one really knows me. In fact, I don't know me. I really have tried to fit in here in Port Byron since I came back. I met Larry in New York when he was working in the New York City Police Department. We met at the Marriott Marquis. We both got drunk and ended up in bed. I loved his toughness and his body. Along with his rough New York accent, he was so different from the Yale guys that I went to school with. We both decided we hated city life, and he took the job as chief of police for Port Byron. I thought going home, being with my mother, would help with my growing depression. We had Stella and Roberta one after another soon after we arrived. Then he found Irene, and soon after, I was in bed with Clarence. I decided I like having many lovers but soon tired of them once I figured I didn't like the hair in their noses or their bodies smelling like horses' feet. And so on and so on. With Larry, he loved to pick his feet just before we made love. That was it. With Clarence, I hardly ever saw him, and after a while I just was not interested in him anymore. We divorced quickly. I needed to find someone else more interesting. Two months later, I discovered this little bar in Auburn called Curley's. I saw some interesting guys there—with good bodies and they were good in bed. I never loved them. I usually told my kids I was going out with the girls but then went out looking for guys. My mother watched them as she stayed up and watched the late night shows. The last guy I met took me to a motel and was a little too rough, but it was okay. When he was asleep, I snuck out. Going out nightly made me so tired the next day that I couldn't give the attention I needed to give to Stella and Roberta. Some days Stella is great and other days she just stares at the wall for hours. I often wonder if she got Asperger's from my genes or Larry's.

Kay, my friend, is driving in this weekend from NYC, and I'm excited to see her and have her talk to me about what kind of life she is living in NYC. I want to tell her everything I'm worried about. I don't like my job of doing brochures or flyers for Good Will, Salvation Army, and other non-profits. It's not challenging or satisfying. I also worry if I would have to move because Larry can't help with more finances. I'm also tired of being lonely and living alone, but I have this need, but there is no one for me. The guys I like never call back, and then there are guys I think I have gotten so drunk they have raped me but everything in the morning was too foggy and I can't report this because Larry would say see I told you so. I also worry about my mom. Yesterday she was clear as a bell until she got up from her nap and thought I was Sister Aloysius, her third-grade teacher. Of course, there is Roberta and Stella. It's all stuff I got to deal with sooner or later.

KAY

I love working for Russ House of Fashion. Being the marketing arm of Russ is what I dreamed of when I was growing up. Even though at times Liz Russ was such a bitch, I like that she has left those stuffy, black pantsuits and sheath dresses behind and her decisions are like the kick-ass, go-getter women we are. Victoria Beckham and Angelina Jolie are the examples. Russ is women's work gear. Personally, I loved wearing mid-prints. I opt for slim, cropped pants and a tailored coat. Anyway, I am looking forward to seeing Bo-Jean. I loved it when we worked together at Russ. We knocked the shit out of everyone in the marketing department. But she thought Larry the cop was going to offer her a better life in that hick town. Then, after the divorce, she met Clarence, a complete uptight preppy type. I also knew that was not going to last. I just don't know how she's coping with Stella's problem and Roberta's silent ways. Then, there is her mother, Anna, with fading memories is also challenging her.

Anna

I don't understand why that kid just stares at the wall and never really answers me when I ask her a question. I think she's retarded, but Bo-Jean says she's a genius and has some special condition. I can't remember the word. In fact, I notice some days, when I try to remember my brothers' names, I can't. I know I had four brothers and only one I can remember is James. My sister, Emma, I can remember, but my brothers' names are lost forever. I hate getting old and depending on Bo-Jean. I wonder where she goes almost every night. I worry about her. I do remember she has brought home some jerks. They all seem like slick dicks. What the hell is my husband's name? He was so nice until the disease got him. I had held his penis when he had to pee. Thank God, he had saved money and invested it. But I don't remember where the money came from. All I remember is that he managed some type of factory that made parts for I don't know. Last night I stayed up most of the night trying to think about that thing you put in a door that opens. At least I have my TV programs. I help with meals, except yesterday I don't know why I had the wooden spoon in my hand. Most of the time I like to sit and think about nothing or my brothers playing with me. What are their names? Then that kid came in and started hitting the wall with her head. Her name I know is Stella. The other one is too quiet, and I never could remember her name. Who is that woman talking to me now?

"Ma, did you eat?"

"Yes."

"What did you have?"

"I forget."

"No, I don't see any dishes in the sink."

"I ate."

"Well," that woman says, "I'm going to fix you some soup. Okay?"

"Okay," I really wish she would go away. I need to go lay down for a while. I'm tired. I need to figure out my brothers' names. Sometimes going through the alphabet helps. Yesterday I couldn't get by *L*.

Bo-Jean

As I walk into the school and head toward Mr. Silverstein's office, I think about his appearance. He was a short ex-marine with steel gray, brushed out hair and a body builder's chest. I am led in to his office as he stands up behind a large, mahogany desk. He motions for me to take a seat in front of the desk.

"Miss Franklin, thanks for coming in," he says sadly. "We really have to deal with Stella's behavior."

"What did she do?" I ask nervously.

"She tried to bite off a boy's ear."

"What happened?"

"I guess this guy Anthony Bucca was kidding her about her always looking like a zonked-out druggie."

"Well, that's not right, even though she takes Adderall. Sometimes she goes into her world."

"I know," he says.

"She should not be made fun of."

"I know," he says with resignation. "But it happened, and Anthony was wrong. However, Stella can't be beating up everyone that looks at her funny or says something to her. You need to talk to her."

"About what?" I say, now defensive.

"To come to me immediately when she feels someone is making fun of her," he says, trying to show empathy. "But she has to control her temper, or next time I'll have to suspend her."

"I'll talk to her," I say, holding back tears. I stand up as he comes around the desk and gently touches my arm. *Understand? Or is he trying to hit on me?*

"Look, I know what it's like coming through a divorce," he says, rubbing my arm affectionately.

Jesus, the jerk is trying to hit on me.

"Maybe we can go out and have a drink sometime."

"Maybe," I say. *Why does every guy want to take care of me? Or fuck me.*

That night I go up to Stella's room. She is sitting in front of her computer, looking at a photo of a high-powered machine gun. I say her name twice, but she doesn't hear until I yell, "Stella!"

She turns quickly with her wide-eyed and virtually translucent eyes. "What?" she asks in her somewhat spaced-out zone.

"Did you try to bite off a guy's ear in school yesterday?" I ask in an understanding tone because anger doesn't work with Asperger's kids.

"I can't remember." She looks like she doesn't know what I'm talking about.

"Look, Stel, if anything happens in school or someone makes fun or belittles you, go to Mr. Silverstein or call me. Understand?"

"Okay," she says passively.

"Do you want to talk about it?"

"No. I am giving a presentation to my history class on high-powered guns."

"Okay, but just call me next time, okay?"

"Okay," she turns and goes back to staring at the computer.

That night, I go out looking for Mister Right, but only find Mister Erectile Dysfunction.

Jeanie

I'm not only worried about Stella but also Bo-Jean. I looked over the Franklin family files. They have an appointment with me in an hour. On occasion I'll meet with them together; sometimes, separately. Last time, I met only with Bo-Jean. She talked to me about a guy she met at a bar and went home with. The guy was rough and punched her all over during their sex. She said she didn't like it, but that's how men are at times. They need to feel powerful and domineering. She said her father used to touch her all over, but it was no big deal. She loved him, and he never hurt her. Then she talked about her daughter Stella's Asperger's. When her daughter Roberta came in alone, she hardly said anything but just sat and listened. She did talk about not liking girls and her classmates. She also talked about feeling more comfortable as a boy. Soon afterwards she said nothing more about the gender issue. Next week I'm meeting with my colleague Ernie Herzberg and plan to talk about the Franklin family. He, like me, is a licensed psychiatrist. Both of us were trained at NYC and our families do things together. My husband, Monte, likes him, and I like his wife, Doris. But I'm getting bored with them. Sometimes I envy the freedom Bo-Jean has in her looking and maybe even in her screwing.

STELLA

At noon I eat my lunch outside near a wooded area away from everyone. And when it's bad weather, I go to the gym and sit up high on the bleachers. I eat the same sandwich every day, turkey on wheat with very little mayo and two Ahoy chocolate chip cookies. I hate the school cafeteria because there are too many people, and I hate the noise of the jerks, especially the nerds who bring their lunches in crumpling paper bags. Most of all, I hate those fluorescent lights and the high frequency sounds when they flicker. The classroom lights I also hate. Their noise is nothing like the fluorescent lights in the cafeteria. Usually I stay wherever I'm at lunch until I hear the bell for my history class. Sometimes I write in a small, black notebook about serial killers I found on the Internet. Recently, I read about Leonarda Cianciulli who lived from 1894 to 1970. She was an Italian serial killer nicknamed the "Soap Maker of Correggio." She murdered three women between 1939 and 1940, turning their bodies into soap and tea cakes, which she would then feed to houseguests. Cianciulli's first two victims were made into tea cakes, consumed by ladies who came to visit, and sometimes she made her kills into soap. She also profited from her crimes, swiping cash and jewelry from her victims. She was tried for murder in 1946 and convicted soon after. Cianciulli was sentenced to thirty years in prison and three years in a criminal asylum, dying behind bars in 1970. I hope I gain notoriety like her.

Today I'm wearing a navy-blue T-shirt and a dress by Mossimo. Mr. Flagg, who teaches the slow students, said I looked good today. No one else ever says anything about my clothes. Everyone thinks I'm weird. Lisa Howard, a cheerleader with a perfect body, called me yesterday an "anorexia sicko." I hate her.

I finish writing in my notebook about Lisa and think I may be putting together a manifesto just like Eric Harris, the Columbine shooter. I like reading and writing in my notebook about serial killers. But I don't write about school shooters. I only read about them. They all seem crazy.

As I walk back to school, I think about what my mother said the other night. She said she had just read that Mozart, Einstein, Andy Warhol, Jane Austen, and even Thomas Jefferson all had Asperger's. I doubt that very much. Did they go crazy like me and break all the windows at Seward School when I was ten? Also, when I really get upset, I rub the rosary beads in my backpack or hanging around my neck inside my dress over and over again, mumbling, "Hail Mary, full of grace. Hail Mary, full of grace, Hail Mary . . ." That cools me down. Even though my mother has been divorced twice, the priests like her. They believe they can save her and perhaps even fuck her. Anyway, I love the bright vestments the priests wear. When the masses are sung in Latin, it makes me think of angels singing. Everything seems right with the world when I'm there. I learned the prayers for mass when my mother sent me to Catholic religious education which I attended when every so often we went to mass. My mom was a drop in Catholic. They were tough years for my mom because she divorced my father, Larry, and then right after that she divorced our absentee stepfather Clarence Asshole. I think my real father Larry still loves my mother but can't understand her need to be free. I wonder if Jeanie is helping. Anyway, for the rest of the day at school I go to classes, but in a sense I'm really situationally retired. I am there physically but mentally thinking of the big day coming soon. I can't wait to see those scared faces and helpless looks of the students, especially because we are considered one of the best high schools in central New York. Right now, I just don't know if I need all those pipe bombs I have. There is so much planning I have to do, even though I have been planning the shooting for months.

Donald Henry Gaskins—The Hitchhiker killer; American. Claims to have killed 100+, but only convicted for 9. Method: torture, mutilation. Started killing in 1969, picking up hitchhikers along coast in the South—averaged one every six weeks—his "fix." Eventually got caught when guy he confided in—a "criminal associate"—saw him murder 2 guys and turned him in to the cops. Sentenced to death, but that got changed to life without parole later. He even managed to kill someone on death row (!). After poisons failed, he rigged up a speaker with C-4, and detonated it when the poor sap thought he'd be communicating with someone in another cell. Clever.

Bo-Jean

I was going to run today. It's Saturday. Usually, when I'm not too hung over, I try to run three miles a day around beautiful and colorful Seward Park. Larry used to worry that someone was going to jump me at the park. So far, no one has jumped me or raped me yet while I'm running, except it's been close with some of my pickups.

As I now begin to run down our driveway in front of our two-story colonial, I see a bright red BMW drive in front of me. *Shit, it's Kay*. I've missed her.

"Hi."

"Hey," she yells, "I thought we would go out this weekend, and you can show me all the good-looking guys in Port Byron." She is my best friend and always dressed perfectly. Stella is so jealous of her but still likes her. She has on a navy skirt with a paperbag waist. Tucked in the skirt is a slim, black turtleneck along with matching Ugg boots. She wears a classic red blazer—the color of her car. Stella and Roberta both like her, especially Stella, because they talk fashion.

She gets out of the car and places her arm around me as we walk into the house.

"Where's the kids?"

"In the kitchen cooking breakfast for us. Basically, it's routine for Saturday morning. You know how Stella likes routine."

"How is she?" She asks more seriously, before we entered the kitchen.

"Other than trying to bite off an ear of a student, she's okay. Thanks for asking."

We enter.

In unison the kids enthusiastically say, "Hi, Aunt Kay."

From a Saks Fifth Avenue bag she pulls out a burgundy sweater suit for Stella and a crisp white pencil skirt for Roberta. Stella loves it, but I can see Roberta is not as happy as she forces a smile. Both of them then leave to go upstairs to their rooms. They are going to try on their new clothes. I'm not sure about Roberta as she still has that forced smile on.

"What you got to drink?" she asks as she searches the pantry, knowing that's where I keep the vodka and gin. She takes out a half of a bottle of vodka, then goes to the refrigerator, takes out a carton of orange juice, gets some glasses, and makes our screwdrivers. I think it will help me get rid of my hangover from last night.

I lead her into the living room.

"Okay, did you find anyone?" Kay asks as she sinks into the brown, overstuffed couch. It is a twelve-foot sectional with corduroy cushions.

"Only guys that want to screw as soon as possible."

"Sounds good. Maybe I should move here. I haven't had sex in weeks. Most of the guys at Russ are gay."

"I know," I say, "but whatever happened to the sexy guys we used to bring in from Italy?"

"Gay."

"Shit no. I can't believe it's almost twenty years since I worked there."

"Yeah. You meet a cop who gets you pregnant and end up barefoot in Port Byron, New York."

"Right."

"You ever see Larry?"

"Not much since he married Extra-Large-Double-X-Boobs Irene, ba-da bing ba-da boom."

"I always told you you needed a breast job."

"Well they're big now but because I'm fat."

"Not fat, just a little plump. Jogging helps you but you got to get on the Mediterranean diet. I lost ten pounds," she says.

"You didn't need to. You were perfect before."

"No. I still got more pounds to go."

"You're crazy. You look great."

"Thanks."

I love having Kay here. I'm glad she comes every few weeks.

Kay and I met when we landed jobs with Russ's marketing department. Liz Russ had just gotten started, and we felt like pioneers in the field of design. Her designs worked for the rich and for the working girl. They were classy, and preppy, but she knew how to use stripes and move beyond the classic knit dresses and pencil skirts. She also always knew what length of skirt would work. I loved her mini-skirts with an edgy leather jacket. Always just right.

When I finished my master's at Yale, I knew I wanted to be in New York. I thought I would get a job at the *Times*, but that was a closed shop, so I was lucky Liz hired both of us. Kay got her master's from NYU, also in literature.

Kay just came over to my desk the first day and said, "I'm Kay Fanning."

"I'm Bo-Jean Franklin," I shook her hand.

"Can I ask you a question?"

"Yes."

"So, do you want to be here?"

"I guess," I said. "It's better than doing ads for a newspaper. You don't know. I may meet Alexander McQueen, Bill Blass, Anna Sui, or maybe even Prada . . . ."

"That's never going to happen."

Kay was always wanting something more. After all, she also really wanted the *Times* and could never accept working for a designer, even though she loved clothes and wanted to wear the newest designer's clothes. Her father owned a chain of car dealerships in New Jersey. He had it all with a big home at Cape May and Naples, Florida. Kay didn't need to work because of her father's money, but she wanted fame in the literary industry. She always wanted guys, a lot of guys who would have sex with her, and to become known in the singles circuit as the new sexual dynamo.

One day she came into the office and said she was bored with writing articles about Liz Russ's poststructural designer mentality.

"Let's blow this place. Russ's craziness, bitchiness, yelling about this is too short, this is not long enough, and I want to kill myself if it doesn't get fit before the show. I'm calling Tom Ford's office. He pays well I heard, and I love his freedom wear."

She grabbed a phone from my desk and dialed.

"Hello, look I'm Tom Ford's friend Holly Peaches. He said if I was willing to work for him, along with Bo-Jangles, he would hire us. Right now we are consulting at Russ House of Fashion. Tell him we are ready to interview. Tell him we met at his Spring Fashion Wear Show."

Quickly I grabbed the phone from her and said, "Are you nuts?"

"Yes," she smiled and then laughed crazily as I hung up the phone. I love her, but at times like then I hated and loved her at the same time. I would never do the things she does, but I envy her because she has the balls to do those things.

My father Fred was like that. He believed in dreams and went after them. His factory made chips for computers, and he had a patent on those chips. I loved spending time with him. He was so kind and understanding. My mother was the strict one.

"Whatever you want, Bo-Jean, daddy will get it," he used to say. "You want the moon, I climb on a beam and get it for you." Being an only child was the best. I looked so forward to when he said to mother and me he was going to sell his factory to Microsoft and we would never have to worry about money for the rest of our lives. But he lost most of it, except he made sure my mother had enough for the rest of her life. The recession hit and she also found out his financial advisor was running a Ponzi scheme, soon retired at fifty-two and died the next year with Alzheimer's and colon cancer. I also think the trial of what happened to me didn't help. I know my problem with men has to be related to what Jimmy Watkins did to me. The scar on my right arm is ugly. He stabbed it with something sharp. They say it was Junior's screwdriver, and I know some guys flinch when they see it when I undress. I worry Jimmy's going to get out soon. Then what?

Roberta

As I sit here in boring social studies class, I think about a story I read on the Internet about Nikki Hayden. I could relate to everything she said about growing up in London. She said she didn't know she wasn't a girl until four or five, where I didn't know I wasn't a boy. She went on to say one of her earliest memories was being yelled at by a teacher for going to the toilet with the girls. About the same age I realized I was different than other girls just like me. And just like me at the age of nine, I wanted my hair cut short. But my mother forced me to have it long. Like Nikki, I get bullied a lot. They pick on me for being too queer, for wearing boys' clothes, for trying to hang around boys, even though they hate me. They mock everything they can think of in terms of gender and sociality. Like Nikki, I learned what trans meant through YouTube. I knew how I felt, but I didn't know there was a term for it.

On a day-to-day basis, I don't tell people I'm transgender because I don't want my mother to find out. She's got enough problems with Stella. I don't wear the beard and sunglasses anymore to the Hot Spot. Because I'm in high school, my mother now lets me wear boys' or men's clothing. In fact, yesterday some woman tried to pick me up at the Hot Spot. I loved her hitting on me. However, I told her I was fucking someone else. In fact, yesterday I won fifty dollars on the slots. I want to get on testosterone and hormone blockers. I have to wear baggy clothes to hide my hips. I have to think about how many layers I have to wear to hide budding tits. I need to learn to be myself and tell my mother about wanting to be a boy. I just want people to accept me as normal in a transgender world. The social studies teacher looks at me funny, so I pretend I am really paying attention and not thinking about being a regular person and a male. I wonder now what would happen if I had let that woman pick me up and she found out my body was a girl's but my mind and soul was a male. I don't know; sometimes I think I want to be a male, but I don't want to get the operation because I want a baby. I wonder if I could find a wife that wouldn't mind. She could have a baby by in vitro.

Larry

Peter Flake comes rushing in with his gray mop of hair going in every direction with eyes bulging and potbelly hanging over his belt.

"You got a minute," he asks.

"Yes." I hated it when he came in always with some problem.

"I just got an email from the State. Did you know Jimmy Watkins is being released this month?" He hands me the email as I think this is not good. I always wanted to kill him because of what he did to Bo-Jean. His family were all white trash. His sister got pregnant when she was fifteen and his brother Frankie is in and out of jail because of drugs. The father was shot by another redneck in a bar fight, and the mother is a drunk. Yesterday, one of my people saw Roberta going into the Hot Spot on Main. He said she seemed dressed like a boy with a baseball hat and baggy jeans. Perhaps if I had stayed, things would have worked out. But Bo-Jean needed several men. However, she is a good mother and loves those kids. I only found out about Jimmy when I asked her about the scar on her arm. She was very vague, but at the office I read the complete file on her trial. Then I understood a little more why I wasn't enough.

Bo-Jean

We are still in my living room. Kay tells me she was promoted to vice-president of marketing. I thought I left because Larry and Port Byron was what I wanted. I was also already a month pregnant with Roberta. Larry wanted us to get married because his parents were strong Catholics. So we got married at St. Rose's in Brooklyn. Larry's father owned a clothing chain of stores that sold slightly defective clothes. He was a multi-millionaire. His mother was a pretty good artist. She only painted sea scenes though.

I can see Kay staring at me now with a look of trouble in her eyes. "So, you're not in love? Bo-Jean, do you hear me?"

"I hear you."

Kay stood up and poured herself more vodka, along with refreshing my glass. I drink it, thinking about Larry and how I blew it. Clarence was a mistake, but Larry I still wanted at times regardless of what happened in the past. I'm tired of being alone all the time. The guys I'm meeting are okay to have sex with but nothing I'm crazy about. There was Ben who is kind but unexciting. I got rid of him fast. I do like Marty. I call him the Italian Stallion, but I think he is going to kill me with his rough sex.

Just then my cell phone rings. It's Larry.

"Hi."

"Hi. Can I come over? It's important."

"You can but Kay is here."

"Well, that's good. I won't stay long. Bye."

"Bye."

I turn to Kay as she is sipping on her drink and asking me who was that on the phone.

"It was Larry, he's coming over."

"Good. I want to see that son of a bitch and ask him how he could leave you with two beautiful kids who need help."

"Kay, let it be," I plead.

An hour later, the doorbell is ringing. Both Roberta and Stella come out of their upstairs cells to see who it is. I open the door and there is Larry in his police chief, tailor-fitted uniform. Still a good looking hulk of a guy with a body builder's posture, huge blue eyes, and short brush-cut of his blond hair. The kids hug him and he tells them he will come up to visit but he has to talk to me first.

After Larry hears their doors closing, he begins to speak.

"I just got word Watkins might get out early. I mean his time is almost up anyway."

"Is that the guy who hurt you years ago?" Kay asks in disbelief.

"Yes, but I don't want to deal with it." Memories begin to wash in from the time he followed me from the classroom to the basement where the boiler room was. I was looking for an exit to get home.

"If he comes around, I'll tell him he's not wanted," Larry says. "His family still lives out Steel Bridge Road. His mother is still alive, along with his brother and sister. I googled the family the other night when I thought his time was getting short." Larry seems worried.

Kay now gets so nervous that she shoves herself out of the sofa and starts to jump up and down in her million-dollar Ugg boots. "Shit! Shit! What if he comes after her, Larry? Then what will you do? Shit!" She whips out her cell phone. "I have a friend in the State. He works for Cuomo."

"Kay, just wait a minute," Larry angrily takes the phone away. "I think I can handle this asshole."

"Please, please," I start crying. "I can't deal with this along with Stella and Roberta." Still standing there at the door, I angrily push Larry aside and swiftly run out towards the woods at the end of the street.

"Where did he touch you, Bo-Jean? Take your time."

"It just hurt."

I keep running until I am in the middle of the woods, exhausted, and in front of me is a small stream where I sit on rocks for a long time, praying someone will hold me again.

Stella

As I leave school and head to where my mom is parked, no one speaks to me, just like any other day. I see kids speaking to Roberta maybe because they don't think she is as weird as me. Soon these stupid people, especially the rich kids, will wish they had spoken to me. I'm invisible to them. Basically, I don't care. I live in my head most of the time, so when people speak to me, I see their lips moving, but I don't hear. Right now, my focus is planning the demise of the school. Eric Harris was a god, like I will be. For once in my life I'll have power and control. I now open the car door and get in.

"Hi," my mother says.

"Hi," I say.

"How was school?" she asks.

"The same."

"Do you mind? I have to stop and get some groceries."

"Fine. I won't go in because . . ."

"I know. I got to fatten you and Roberta up."

As I wait in the parking lot of Wegmans, I think about how I used to have a friend. Her name was Mary Ann, but she moved away. That's the last and only friend I had. I thought someday I could work something up with her, but I could never have a sexual experience with anyone because of the touching thing. But I liked walking in the woods with her and talking about deep thoughts: Is there a God? What happens to us when we die? We both felt nothing happens to us except becoming piles of leftover atoms, neutrons, and electrons after death. Our discussions were far ahead of what we talked about in school.

All these assholes in school just want to talk about who is going out with whom after the football game. My mother keeps saying I don't try to make friends, but I do, and time after time they reject me.

So every day I follow the schedule; however, when the day is chaotic or there is too much noise in my head, I just sit at my desk, touch the rosary beads on my chest, and repeat over and over, "Hail Mary, full of grace. Hail Mary, full of grace." But when there are too many conversations in the hall before class, I freak out. That's why I never eat there because of the noise and lights. Also, the noise in the cafeteria when everyone is talking at the same time drives me crazy. I look forward to going to class because it's only one teacher talking. I especially like it when the teacher just lectures and doesn't interact with students. If it gets too loud in the hall, I wear earplugs. I tried wearing earphones with them turned off, but my mother said I looked stupid.

Bo-Jean

I came back to the house and find my mother cooking soup. Kay and Larry are gone.

"Want some?" she asks.

"Not really, Mom, but I want to ask do you remember all the stuff I went through with Jimmy Watkins?"

"Who?"

"Jimmy Watkins, you know, the kid that did the stuff to me in seventh grade."

"I think," she says as she looks confused, "did you go out with him?"

"Mom, never mind."

"Well, your father took care of those guys you went out with."

"Right." I think how upset he was and wanted to kill Watkins, especially at the trial. My mother never came because she said she was too nervous.

"That's okay, Mom. I'm going up to my room and lie down. I have to go to a meeting tonight."

"Go rest. You look tired."

"Okay." I leave and go up and try to block out Jimmy Watkins.

ANNA

I pour myself some soup in a bowl, thinking, why should I remember Jimmy Watkins? Maybe Bo-Jean should've married him instead of who is that. I do need to remember better. Everything seems to be erasing from my mind. I keep telling Bo-Jean that she's never going to find the perfect match. I was lucky with Fred. Only once in a blue moon will that happen. Fred loved Bo-Jean and she loved him. Perhaps they were too close. I wonder when Fred is coming home tonight. I feel so stupid at times. Who are the kids in the house? One is a boy, I think, and the other is nice, but I think she is retarded. Did I have a son named Mark, and where is he? Or did he die at birth? I must concentrate better because that woman upstairs can be mean. She hit me yesterday with a razor strap or was it a wooden soup spoon. I must stop thinking and make my mind go blank. I wonder about my brothers. I need to wash the bowl now and lay down because my head hurts. Whose house is this? Who's that woman upstairs? I haven't seen her before. I must tell her to leave later. I don't want my mother to know her. I hope that nice man who comes and goes will come back. I really like him, but I must not let him kiss or fiddle around with my body. I'm a good girl and not sassy like my sister Florence who puts out for all the guys. I don't like playing with myself, but I know that little boy wants to put his hands in there because the way he looked at me when I came out of the bathroom. He rubbed my breasts when I laid down and I know he liked it. He's a nice boy but how many sisters or brothers I have. A, B, C, D, E, . . . and how could that be I forgot the rest. Heck, that can't be I have a degree from Wellesley. I go upstairs. Which door is mine? That one to the left. I open it, and there is a body on my bed. No, I'll go to other room There the cross is on the wall. I lay down, praying Sweet Jesus please turn off my mind.

Bo-Jean

I told Larry I would meet him at the Carriage House in Seneca Falls tonight because I want to see if that good-looking guy will be there at the bar. I know we can connect, but the last time I was into a guy I thought would be good in bed all he talked about at his place was his business and about not being able to get his thing up because his ex-wife made fun of him in bed.

Tonight I dress up in that black, tight cocktail dress with a double strand of white pearls and pearl earrings. I tease my hair into tresses, and I think I look seductive, even though I have put on weight since we were married. I want to be attractive to Larry, but I want the other guy tonight. The other guy looks like Ryan Gosling with a more defined nose and mouth. This guy is sexy like Ryan too.

Most of the time I get an Uber in case we end up here in my bedroom, or the Ryan Gosling look-alike goes for me and we go to his place. I really need no romance tonight, but I need just pure sex and fifty or more orgasms.

The Carriage House sits on the far end of Seneca Lake, one of the most charming Finger Lakes. As I walk in, Larry waves to me at a table he has. I look over to the bar and see that Ryan Gosling isn't yet there. It is still early. Guys like him show up late to be cool.

As I approach the table, Larry gets up and gives me a stiff hug. It is so fake. I wonder why.

"Hi," he says.

"Hi."

He sits as I sit across from him.

"Look, I just didn't want to talk about the whole Jimmy Watkins thing with Kay there and all. I'm sorry I got into all of it."

"I understand but I don't know if I want to talk about it yet." I say, standoffishly.

"Well, let me tell you what we know."

"Okay." *I remember, and I'm not sure if it was Jimmy or Junior Washington, but he was really heavy as I fought him. He was too strong, too. He turned me over, and as he put his hand over my mouth, I bit him. Bleeding, he aggressively pulled my pants down. Then I just remembered yelling, "Please don't, don't. I won't tell anyone. Please stop."*

Larry continues to talk. "Well, he is definitely getting out in a few days from now. And he is coming back here because of a sister and brother."

"So what do I do?" *It was really Junior Washington.*

"Get a lawyer and try to convince a judge you want a lifetime restraining order for Jimmy. They say now he found Jesus in prison."

Dazed, I push the table away. "Larry, I'm sorry I can't deal with this now. I appreciate it." Everyone is looking at me as I rush out and walk to a small convenience store. Looking out the store's door, I wait for Larry to leave and then go back in to wait for Ryan Gosling. I need to forget and I know good, hard sex will help.

Sitting at the bar, drinking vodka on the rocks, Ryan Gosling comes in and sits next to me.

"Hi, Chet Kinney," he says, shaking my hand.

"Bo-Jean Franklin."

"What do you do?" he asks, ordering a Bud Light. Now the game begins. The Hunt, Ernest Hemingway said, is the beginning.

"I work for a printer in graphics and write text. What about you?"

"City attorney for Seneca Falls. I've seen you here a few times. Are you free tonight?"

"I'm free all the time and free from the world," I say flippantly.

"Good." He is served his Bud Light.

"Want to get out of here?" I ask, leaning my breasts into him. "I've had a tough day."

"How about my place?" he asks.

"Sure. You're not married, are you?" I ask.

"No, I was but that was over five years ago." He pays the bill and we leave.

Jeanie

"Are you feeling okay? You seem down." This is probably the third session I had with Roberta, and I can't seem to crack the shell.

"Yes," she answered in a flat-toned voice.

"How are you getting along with your mom?"

"Okay."

I know she wants to be someplace else. There seems no affect. I have other teenagers like her. They are so into the social media world they don't know how to sustain a conversation.

"Do you want to be here, Roberta?"

"No," she says, emotionless.

"Well, I've got forty minutes to go. I know you're a senior. Are you making any plans for next year?"

"No."

"What would you like to do five years from now?"

"I don't know."

"Do you want to go to college?"

"I think."

"What do you want to study?"

"I don't know, maybe writing."

"You want to go on and get a degree in literature like your mother?"

"No."

"Why?"

"Heck, she's forty and doesn't know yet what she wants."

"You want to talk about that?"

"No."

"Do you and your mother get along? I know I already asked that."

"I don't know but I think I have a better relationship with my grandmother even though sometimes she forgets my name. She's so nice and understanding."

"You think your mother isn't nice and understanding?"

"I don't know."

"Maybe next time we can talk more about your relationship with her."

"I don't care."

She gets up and leaves as I write in her file: "For the most part unresponsive but perhaps there is something there about her relationship with her mother and grandmother."

Anonymous text [to Roberta]: *He/She/It whatever you are, queer.*

Bo-Jean

It is your typical suburban two-story home, colonial with white shutters. Almost a carbon copy of mine in Port Byron. He leads me into the living room and asks, "Want a drink?"

"Any white wine would be fine."

"Okay."

He goes into another part of the open living room to the kitchen area and takes a bottle of wine from the refrigerator, then he takes two glasses from the cupboard and pours two glasses. He hands me a glass and motions for me to sit on a light blue sectional sofa.

"As I've said, I've noticed you before at the Carriage. You go there often?"

"Sometimes." *Where else are you going to go to pick up some-one? Seneca Falls is closer than Syracuse.* I did the Syracuse thing a couple times, and still I can't remember how I got back home. One guy left me with a bloody nose and I remembered police coming to the door and asking if everything was all right because a neighbor called and said they heard yelling. I don't remember any of that. Lately, if I drink too much, I can't remember any-thing. Total blackout. I wondered why Larry never called about that night. I know his officer must've told him.

"Are you married?" he asks.

"Was twice."

"Sorry to hear that," he says as he starts to rub the outside of my dress down there. I feel heat spreading throughout my body. He takes my glass of wine from me and places it on a huge round coffee table in front of us. And before I know it, he's got my dress off and is kissing my breasts and then he suddenly yells.

"No no!" He pushes hard against me and then releases. His pants are still on.

"I'm so sorry, it's something I take pills for."

Angrily, I now push him off me, pulled up my dress, and run out the door, called and got an Uber home.

As I quietly walk into the house that night, I see my Mother on the sofa, looking at the TV. I think it's the Catholic station with a nun who has a twisted face repeating the words, "Jesus will guide you just turn yourself to him."

"Mom!" I yell.

She doesn't hear me at first, so I yell again.

"Mom!"

She turns around in that dazed state she often goes into now.

"Mom, you okay?"

Finally, she speaks "What? Yes, I'm okay. How about you?"

"I'm fine," I lie, as I think that my Ryan Gosling needs help. I go around and sit next to her on the sofa.

"Mom, are you doing okay?"

"Yes, why do you ask?"

"Well, I don't know, sometimes I think you seem like in a different world."

"I know, I just got to concentrate better."

"Shouldn't we go to the doctor and have you checked?"

"Maybe next month. Right now, I am doing fine."

"But, Mom, you're not."

"I know how I feel."

I get up, still feeling the aftereffects of pre-ejaculation Chet.

"Okay, I'm going to bed, but please, if you're not feeling well, please tell me."

"I will, Bo-Jean. Remember what I said about once in a blue moon?"

"Yes," I say, thinking I'm too tired to talk.

"Okay, honey, remember it's hard to find the right man."

"I know, Mom. I know!" Do I know, but that's fine with me. She remembered my name.

That night I fall asleep thinking of Steve Stemplin, whom I met at Curley's the other night. He seemed nice. He was a professor at Auburn Community College. Perhaps I will go there tomorrow and see if he's around. I know I'm getting rough around the edges. Sometimes it makes me hard and bitter. I don't like living without someone to love me anymore. I feel very sad, lonely, hurt, and depressed. Yesterday I took a depression checklist, and I was "all of the above." That scares me.

STELLA

After we get back from the store, I help my mom carry in the groceries, and then I tell her I have some homework to do in my room. Tonight I need to sneak out after she goes out. The storage unit is about a mile away. When I'm having a wild day, I go there to space out.

I know my mother is hurting after two divorces, but I don't always understand her body language. That's quite normal for someone with Asperger's. It is pointless to expect me to look at her and know how she is feeling simply because her smile is too tight or she is hunched over and hugging her arms to herself. Just as it would be pointless to expect a deaf person to hear a voice.

My mother is always complaining that I have no interests. But I do. I like my guns, and I like it when we go together to the shooting range. I'm a pretty good shooter. My mother told me that I should see when I'm ready if I can get a scholarship for shooting at a university. She heard West Virginia University has an excellent team. In fact, a female from their team just won an Olympic medal. Anyway, I know she would go apeshit if she knew I had all of that stuff in the storage unit. I think like Eric Harris, and I will wear the duster with a black turtleneck, and black pants, shoes, and even underwear—all black. I want to look good when they carry me away.

I am going to place the bombs in the bathrooms and then set them off by a timer. I also think because it is April. That's when Columbine, Oklahoma City, and the Boston bombing took place.

I think I've learned a lot about hydrazine, perchlorate, and nitro-glycerin. The Internet has been great in teaching me about elements for bomb making. I'm not sure how many knives to bring, though. I'll be like Eric Harris, but one of the first female shooters in the world. All the girls will want to know everything about me.

I hope they find my little black notebook.

Tsutomu Miyazaki—the Human Dracula, The Otaku Murderer, The Little Girl Murderer, Dracula Miyazaki; Japanese. 1988–89: abducted and killed 4 little girls, then would molest their corpses. Once, drank some of his victim's blood and ate part of her hand. He'd write to families of his victims with details of what he did—you got to keep good records—and harass them with silent phone calls. His father committed suicide in 1994. Miyazaki was hanged 6/17/08, age 45.

Bo-Jean

Larry texts: *We need to talk again. He's getting out in exactly 15 days. What do you want to do?*

I text back: *Right now, as I said, I can't deal with it. Leave me alone.*

Larry texts: *Think about our kids, your mother. I can't find a way for him to never come back to Port Byron.*

I decide not to respond. I thought now about Mark Stacy in the fifth grade. He really was my first love. Even now, my face gets hot thinking about him. I remember one morning about a year ago getting a call from his best friend, Eddie Bell.

"Did you know Mark Stacy died?"

"No. The last time I heard from him was several years ago when I was working in New York."

"Well, I thought you might want to know. I know you were close to him when we were in school." I remember dreams about him that helped me forget Jimmy for a while.

"Thanks, Eddie." I hung up the phone. *Shit, I should've asked how he died.* I also remembered when we met in the fifth grade.

The principal at Seward school called my parents and asked them to come in. Her name was Mrs. Bush. At the school, they were *Downton Abbey* types who loved my father because he was well-respected throughout the community. My mother was invisible in their eyes. They said they thought I was very bright but unable to stay out of trouble. However, the major reason my parents were asked to come in was because I had loosened some nuts on the teachers' commode so that when they flushed, instead of the water going down, it shot up like a geyser. I hid across the hall behind a half-opened door and watched with glee as the women, especially Mrs. Bush, came out, angrily shaking their dresses. Mrs. Bush told my parents that I was too much to handle and suggested that Seymour Street School had teachers better suited for discipline problems.

The following fall and for the fifth grade I went to Seymour Street School where I met Mark. Seymour Street School was an elementary school (K–5) and a middle school (6–8). I was given a seat in back of him, and as I approached him, his big brown eyes, long eyelashes, and wide grin warmed me all over. I knew something good would come of us. While I passed him on my to my seat, I noticed his well-built body underneath his blue shirt. I was quiet all day, staring at his bluish-black, curly hair on his neck. I was in love, and it would be forever. But the problem was I was too shy to talk to him for any extent of time. He was my dreamboat guy. We never really got close until my mother forced me to attend a Fall teen dance at the Sullivan Rec Center. After the dance, he asked me if he could walk me home. I said yes, and on the way home he kissed me in front of my house, and until what happened in the boiler room we were boyfriend and girlfriend.

He was a beautiful person, an angel who would have a handprint on my heart forever. However, I could never face him again because I was too ashamed and guilty because of Jimmy and Junior.

ROBERTA

I got to the Hot Spot after school. I had cut my hair like business-
men do. Short and butch-like. Anyway, Amy, who owns the Hot
Spot, has taken a liking to me. I help in the kitchen, wait on people, and clean up when she tells me. I can play the games as much
as I like, but of course I can't win anything.

Amy has asked me to come home with her, but I think she is
looking for something more than friendship. I'm not ready for
that kind of stuff yet. I also still don't know exactly what I am at
times. Like now, I want to be a male, but other times I feel asexual
and aromantic. I just want to be me. I think one's gender or sexuality can change over a lifetime. Perhaps when I'm thirty I'll like
something else, or I'll be neutral.

I sweep up the floors from the older people and welfare recip-
ients who come in during the day. Today, there are about three of
us in the place. Two retired factory workers and an older lady who
comes in every day and spends twenty dollars on the slots. She'll
sip on one gin and tonic the whole time. I go over to see if she
needs anything.

"I'm okay," she says.

"Okay."

"Robert, do you have any grandparents?"

"Just my grandmother Anna. The others are in New York City
and I really don't know them."

"Do you talk to her?"

"Sometimes, but because of school and this place, I don't
have a lot of time."

"Make time," she says as she pulls down the slot arm and comes up with only two oranges.

"You see, our generation is afraid of the weapon of mass destruction, Alzheimer's. It's like genocide. It eventually gets you. It's winning and that's why many people are committing suicide. The only people getting rich on us is our doctors, and the hospitals, nursing homes, and hospice groups. We're dying little by little while living. You understand, Robby?"

"I think."

"Well, if you don't see me around for a couple of days, you know then it's got me."

"Don't say that. You look great and you're going to live a long time."

"I'm telling you, this is the new Holocaust except it's not Jews, but anyone older than sixty."

She pushes down the arm and comes up with nothing. She gets up, finishes her drink, smiles at me, and leaves.

ANNA

After Fred died, I went to an assisted living facility called Oakdale. I didn't really want to go, but I could see Bo-Jean was having a lot of problems. I didn't want to be another problem. Even though Fred lost money near the end, he left me enough so I would have money for an Oakdale-type place. I also had private caregivers during the day because just before Fred died I broke my hip and had it replaced. In fact, I never made it to Fred's wake or funeral because of the pain.

Oakdale, on the outside, was beautiful. It had a large pond with ducks in it and also lovely flowers and trees and landscaping around the front entrance. But inside was something else. There were all sorts of rules and schedules. At times, I thought it was a glorified prison. You had to eat at a certain time, you couldn't stay up past ten o'clock, and you had to be at certain activities like card making and singing, regardless of whether or not you were interested.

Those first few months I was in terrible pain and needed help with walking and eating. I would become upset if the nurses didn't bring my pain pills. My private care nurses were stupid. Many times if I didn't like them, I would fire them.

Bo-Jean would get mad. "Mom, we are running out of caregivers to take care of you."

"I don't care. They are stupid, and I don't like lazy ones, especially that Donna who has missing teeth and lives in a trailer. I wish I could fire some of the Oakdale nurses. At night they never check on me."

"I'll talk to them, but you can't be mean to them. You understand?"

"I don't care. They are supposed to check on me all night and give me pain pills. Also, I don't know why I have to sit with certain people at dinner when I don't like them. They won't let me bring my food to my room."

"Because they want you to socialize and make friends."

"Okay. I'll try to do better. Still I hate lazy people and also they want me to be docile and get ready for death. They call it getting ready to go home. That's bullshit."

"Mom, listen, after I see you, I'm supposed to go see Kathy Taylor, the Executive Director of Oakdale."

"Why?"

"I don't know. But please be good."

"Okay, but they better be good to me."

After Bo-Jean left, I thought about how the residents all think their shit doesn't stink and pretending they're in a country club when really it's a place getting ready for us to die. But here, if they know you may have a terminal disease they want you out. For Oakdale administrators, they want everyone to think that death doesn't exist.

BO-JEAN

After my father died, my mother tried living at home with care-givers coming in every few days, but it didn't work. I think she really missed my father because he did so many things for her. He waited on her hand and foot. Everything had to be perfect for her. Once she broke her hip, it seemed like she needed constant attention. Before the hip replacement she would walk three or five miles a day. But the accident made her more aware of her mortal-ity, and she was afraid of being left alone at night. However, when she stopped cooking for herself, I had to move her to assisted living. She used a walker, and the staff at Oakdale thought she would fit in nicely. So, as I entered the luxuriously carpeted lobby of Oakdale, with all its huge leafy plants and flowery wallpaper, I wondered why Kathy Taylor wanted to see me. As I waited in the lobby, Kathy Taylor came out to get me. Dyed blonde hair, a huge chest, and a somewhat plump body greeted me as she led me into her office. I hated her false smile as she talked about the weather and the ducks in the pond.

Then she started. "Mrs. Franklin, we have a problem with your mother," she said quite seriously.

"What is it?"

"She is constantly calling for the nurses to come to her room. Yesterday it was twenty-five times. We just don't have the staff to do that."

"I understand."

"Basically, it is usually nothing except to see if they will come. She also has all those private caregivers."

"I can talk to her."

"Well, it's more than that. If your mother doesn't like the nurses or aides because they're black, overweight, foreign, and so forth, she tells them to leave and send someone else. In fact, I went in this morning to talk to her about the constant calling, and the dismissing staff with prejudice. So when I was finished talking to her about these behaviors, she dismissed me, 'You may go now. I've heard enough.'"

I could feel myself getting angry. "Are you saying she is the only one that does this?"

"I'm sorry, but yes. Your mother is one of a kind and if she doesn't stop bothering my staff, she'll have to go."

I got up quickly and full of emotion, and said, "She will be out of here in the next hour."

I heard her say behind my back, "Mrs. Franklin, please let's see if we can work something—"

That's the last I heard as I slammed the door behind me.

STELLA

Today I thought how the devil is really God. I must write that in my little black book. I also must put in that killing is good because that's the devil's work. If he is God, then it's good. Anyway, after I hear my mother coming in around three, I wait about thirty minutes and quietly go down the stairs and go out the front door. It only takes me fifteen minutes to arrive at the storage unit. Except for a few streetlights it is nearly all black. I take out my flashlight and quickly open the padlock. Once inside, I shine the light on an assortment of boxes and containers that I worked on this past year. There are also roof cement, about four Styrofoam coolers, a box of ammunition, three pipe bombs, two camouflage bags, three pressure cookers, an SKS assault rifle with sixty rounds of ammunition, a Beretta 9 mm hand gun, a .22 caliber rifle, and an assortment of knives. I know I am not going to use all of this for tomorrow's shootings. But I know I am going to use the .22 on someone special. I place the Beretta and .22 caliber rifle along with the pipe bomb in one of the two camouflage bags. The knives I'll bring along just in case I'm jumped.

I got the guns, knives, and bomb stuff from Big Red. Everyone in Port Byron gets guns from him. He's a big burly guy with a red, straggly beard. I heard he gets all his stuff from gun shows and sells it out of his storage unit, which is three doors down from mine.

Today at school I tried sneaking in a side hallway. I was hoping the bell for school had already rung, but there are two boys there who look like seniors. I've never seen them before. One is tall and fat, and the other is thin with a lot of pimples on his pale-looking face. I try walking quickly by as they yell, "fucking queer, suck my cock." Then both grabbed me and spit in my face. The big one slams my head against the lockers while the other one kicks me in my crotch. Both are laughing as I run to math class. Their saliva is running down my face, mixing with my tears.

Nannie Doss—Giggling Granny, Lonely Hearts Killer, Black Widow, Lady Blue Beard; American, born 1905. Seems to have enjoyed killing husbands and relatives.

First married when 16. Unhappy marriage to Charley Braggs, but 4 kids. Braggs didn't leave her until after middle 2 daughters died: so-called "food poisoning," but probably killed by Doss. Doss and Braggs both slept around a lot. He was the lucky one that got away.

Remarried in 1929, to Robert Harrelson. This one lasted 16 years. She killed her 2 little grandsons for the insurance money. Harrelson, drunk, raped her in 1945. After that, she added rat poison to his booze, which took care of him.

Number 3: Arlie Lanning. Married 3 days after meeting. He was another drunk; she'd run off for long periods. He dies of "heart failure," and then their house burned down. More insurance cash for her.

The 4th hubby died too, of course. Doss's mom came to live with her. Predictably, she was poisoned too.

Fifth and final husband: Samuel Doss. Ended up in hospital w/ digestive tract infection, killed by Nannie night he was released—had to hurry up and collect on those life insurance policies. His doctor got suspicious, and they found arsenic during autopsy.

She was rounded up, and confessed to killing: 4 husbands, mom, sister, grandsons & mother-in-law. Sentenced to life, 1955; died of leukemia in prison, 1965.

Bo-Jean

Tonight, I decided to go to Curley's. The last time, I met a nice guy who was a great kisser. I was hoping that guy would be there. On the way there I thought about Mark Stacy. I can't believe he's dead. I missed seeing Mark and looking at his big brown eyes and that wide, seductive grin. I loved him deeply and sometimes became thrilled when I got a Valentine's card that said "love you," which I knew he sent to all the girls.

I open the door to Curley's and see a good looking guy sitting there at the bar. He was tall, well built, and had great blue eyes. He smiles as I approach and pray that tonight I will meet my Prince Charming. As I take a seat next to him, he asks, "What do you want to drink?"

"Oh," I say, half listening. "Sorry. I was thinking about something else but I'm back. Vodka Collins, thanks."

"You okay?"

"I'm fine, just fine," I lie. Hopefully tonight, I think, you will be the one.

"You just seem a little out of it."

"I'm fine. Really I'm fine." I lie again.

"Would you like to go to my condo? It's two blocks from here. I'll drive. Maybe it will help you relax a little."

"Sounds good."

We finish our drinks, leave, and head toward his place. When he opens the door to his living room, it seems to have very little furniture. Sofa, lamps. Coffee table, and I can see his bedroom down the hall. Everything seems neat.

"Do you want a drink?" he asks.

"Sure. Another vodka Collins is fine." I was starting to feel a little drunk from the drink before but feel sexy now.

He brings the drinks over as I sit on the sofa with him next to me. I think he is drinking white wine.

"Do you have any children?" he asks.

"Two teenage girls," I say as I sip on my drink. It seems strong. I just want to forget Larry, Jimmy Watkins, Junior, and all that shit.

"I have three, two boys and a girl. They're all teenagers," he says. "A few months ago, I got a divorce."

"Sorry to hear that," I say.

"I had been married for twenty years, but I was just looking for something more from our marriage. She was a very strict Baptist. Also, her father was a preacher."

"Doesn't sound good," I say, as I lean back on the sofa.

"All I wanted was to have more fun with sex. I think she hated it," he says as he begins rubbing my leg and moving my skirt up. I like him. "You divorced?"

"Twice."

"What happened?"

"My one ex didn't like that I wanted to be free. The other was never home."

"That's a bitch. Do you work now?" he asks.

"I'm a writer but right now I help out with marketing at a printing company. I used to work for a major designer in New York."

"I'm impressed. Want some weed?" he asks.

"I don't care," I say.

He gets up, goes to his bedroom, and brings two joints out. He lights both as he hands me one. When he sits down now, he begins to massage my breasts as I take a drag on the joint. I am completely relaxed. He still continues to talk about his ex and him.

"I started to go out with one of my students who worked for me at Auburn Community. We dropped acid and did cocaine. I liked it. But one night I got home, and my wife had her father the preacher and his wife there, and they started examining me about the kind of life I was leading. I asked them to leave so I could talk to my wife, Tyler. They wouldn't go. Finally, I just told them your daughter hates sex but I like it and I want to do things like have a little weed so we can be like other couples in this world. That was it. They left and the next day she asked me for a divorce."

Still on the sofa, he begins to kiss me hard as he got on top of me and somehow we both get undressed and he comes quickly.

We both fall asleep afterwards until I feel his hand shaking my shoulder.

"Bo-Jean, you got to go," he says.

Still in a drunken haze, "What, what time is it?" I ask, slurring my words.

"Three thirty," he says somewhat coldly. "You got to go."

"Okay," I say as I began to dress. "Is there something wrong?" I ask.

"No, just sometimes one of the kids stops by on the way to school," he says with emphasis.

"Okay."

I leave. Like so many other guys, I wait weeks, hoping he will call. I like him. He never does.

JEANIE

Today, I wanted Bo-Jean to deal with Jimmy Watkins. She sat across from me on the sofa. I sat on a multi-colored, wingback chair. Every time I bring his name up, she won't respond. Larry Myers knows I have been working with her for a while. In fact, I worked with them both when they were having problems with their marriage, so I know a little about Jimmy. He called me yesterday and told me more about what he knew about Jimmy Watkins. He thought I needed to deal with it now because Jimmy was getting out soon. But first I'll deal with the kids and her mother then slowly bring the subject up.

"How are things going?" I ask.

"Okay I guess," she says as if I was bothering her.

"How's the kids and Mom?"

"Look, I am feeling depressed today. Do we have to talk about these things?" she responds with a little agitation.

"Several years ago you came to me."

"You're right. I just didn't know what to do with Stella and Roberta," she says, more engaged. "Things seem a little bit better with Stella now that I am involved with her and going to shooting practice together."

"Good," I say. I'm still worried about guns in Stella's hands.

"How's your mother doing?" I ask.

"I don't know. Some days she seems with it and other days she seems spaced out. Like yesterday she asked if my dad was coming to visit, and when I said he's no longer with us, she seemed not to conceptualize what I said. But today she seems to be in this world."

"That's how that disease works, and slowly she will be gone to that other world for good," I say, reaching out and touching her hand. "And Roberta is okay?"

"Yeah, but she seems to be in her own little world, too."

"I agree with you. I think she's still trying to figure out where she belongs," I say, thinking about her identity problems. "And now shouldn't we talk about Jimmy Watkins and his getting out in a few days?" I ask as her body seems to become rigid.

"I just don't want to think about it. Look, I know some of my problems I had with my marriages and men were because of what happened. As I told you when we first met, I just don't want to deal with all of that."

"Why don't you want to talk about it?" I ask. "I think maybe that is related to what you are doing at night."

"I know. Look, the other night I met a guy, and I thought he wanted to date me but he never called. I get restless at night, and I have to get out but hate the idea of whoring around."

"Why?" I ask, hoping that we're getting someplace. However, she stands up and becomes disconnected from me.

"I gotta go. I have to pick up Stella from school."

I look at my watch and say we still have another ten minutes.

"Sorry. I gotta go," she says.

"I just want to know what it is like to love somebody with every fiber of your being. I've read that in so many books. To love someone with every fiber of your being. I think that's what I had with this Scott Shaw at Yale. But he didn't love me like that."

She goes out the door as I wonder what it would be like to whore around with her.

ROBERTA

As I sit in a boring history class about the causes of the Civil War, I start to write a letter to my mother. I have to do something. Yesterday afternoon I almost went home with Amy. She tenderly kissed me in the storage room where I was getting more napkins. I got scared because I liked it but went quickly back to see if anyone wanted a drink or something to eat.

I now write: "Mom, what am I? You see, Mom, I ask myself this all the time. I really believe I'm a boy in a girl's body. That's it. It's not your fault. It just is. I thought at some time I could talk to Larry, but being a cop, he's too macho. I can't quite explain it. It is just a feeling of being not quite in my body. I mean, I appreciate you and Dad, as long as he was with us. He made me feel that both Stella and me, even with Stella's problems, could do everything that boys could do. I just want to tell you that I started to feel awkward and uncomfortable when my breasts began to grow and I began to bleed. I didn't like it and when I went on the Internet I understood I was transgender. You see, that's why I got my hair cut and I wear a Lyco vest that painfully flattens my chest. I want to be seen as a male. I want the world to see me as I am beginning to see myself. I love you, Roberta." Someday, I'll give it to her.

LARRY

This morning, I waited in the visitor's room of the Auburn State Prison, a few miles from Port Byron. It's painted institutional gray with gray metal tables and chairs. The guard was dressed in khaki pants and shirt. He stands against the wall as Jimmy Watkins talked. I noticed Jimmy's hair is all steel gray. He is solidly built with a square face and huge, green eyes.

"Jimmy, do you know why I'm here?"

"Yeah, because of Bo-Jean," he said matter-of-factly.

"Look, I know you're getting out in a few days."

"Yeah, I am. Twenty years here is too much," he said angrily.

"Are you planning to come back to Port Byron?" I asked.

"Yeah, my sister still lives there and also my brother who has cancer."

"Well, I would hope you would stay away from Bo-Jean."

"I heard you married her and had a couple of kids, then dropped her," he smiled sarcastically.

"That's not true," I said, pissed. "I just want you to know if you get near her or my kids you will be back in here in a minute."

"Look, that's over, we were kids. I served my time for what I did to her. Junior Washington really did it, but he's dead. He got what he deserved. I served my time—first at Elmira because of my age and then here. It's over and you can tell your ex-wife she knows it was Junior that fucked her, not me. I just watched and had fun with myself."

I quickly got up, but the guard came over and placed his hand on my shoulder and said, "That's it, officer." Jimmy laughed coldheartedly as he was led out.

"Asshole," I murmured under my breath. I don't care who did it. *I hate him with a passion.*

ANNA

I miss my husband's arms holding me. I think as I take the clothes out of the dryer and fold them. I want to help Bo-Jean, who seems so lost. But some days I feel so drained and all I want to do is to dream about days gone by. I hardly sleep anymore, as I just wait here, waiting for death. But I have to hang on for Bo-Jean and the kids. She won't accept that it only happens once in a blue moon. Fred and I had it. I have started to forget people's names, and I work the alphabet over and over and I can't remember them. What is the name of Bo-Jean's youngest? She wanted to know if I knew the name of the store where they sell sexy underwear for women. I couldn't remember and still I'm completely blank on the name. I'll think about it and hopefully it comes tonight. I can't even get by *E* in the alphabet now, trying names out. I think she was just checking to see if I had lost all my memory. She wasn't the type to wear those things.

STELLA

I am walking from my favorite lunch spot near the woods and noticed that there are a bunch of students near the entrance door. For some reason, lunch is later today. With my head down, I try walking by them until Marty Glick stops me. He is on the football team. I think he plays quarterback. He has a round face and loads of curly, blond hair with big brown eyes.

"Hey, what are you doing in the woods?" he asks as he grabs and holds my wrist.

"Nothing. Please, I have to get to class," I say, as I feel his grip getting tighter.

"What's wrong with you anyway? Don't you like guys? Maybe you're a lesbian, huh?"

"Please let me go," I say. I would love to blow his head off. Everyone starts laughing as he lets me go and pushes me into the door. As I go to math class, I think about using the .22 on him and all those laughing at me. Maybe even stabbing the shit out of them. My mother doesn't know about the .22 I have at home along with the other guns in the closet. I know my mother keeps one handgun in her nightstand. My father thought it important. He is a good father, and I just wish I saw him more than two weekends a month. His new wife tries hard with Roberta and me. I just can't get close to her because of my problem. She talks too fast, and she looks like a prostitute sometimes.

Now Mr. Walters is talking about quadratic equations, so I start to dream about the day the world will know my name. Tonight I will carry the camouflage bags and go through the side door of the gym, which I know will be open because the jocks use it sometimes late at night for practice. I hope I see them tomorrow because it will be "Hasta la vista, Baby." Stupid jerks, I still don't get the basketball game of putting a ball in a basket. I'll place the bags under the bleachers. I'll do that early in the morning. Then I'll take the pipe bombs out. Thinking about every detail, I'll run to the first floor bathrooms and place the bombs in the stalls with their timers set for 7:15 AM. I can't wait to shoot someone tomorrow in the head and see their blood and muscles splattered all over. As I listen to Mr. Walters go on and on, I think he will be the first to go. I will shoot him in his beer gut and watch him gurgle blood and phlegm. He is so stupid like most of the teachers, except for Mrs. Cronin, my English teacher. I love her interpretations of poems, but she'll also have to die. All of them will have to die. Also, I can't wait to shoot out all the fluorescent lights. I hate them. Another thing that is crazy is I love darkness and the number 999. I also love the letters *w* and *x*. I don't know why. I just do. But I know I have to do all of this so that the world can become safe. I think I will go to the library first. Here I will use my 9 mm Hi-Point 995 carbine. I'll begin shooting at the few nerds there studying. When I shoot, I'll yell, "May the Lord bless you." I will ask them if they believe in God. I remember reading another shooter doing the same thing. If they say yes, I'll say, "Too bad. The devil is my God." I hope I break the record for school shootings. I think Eric would be so proud of me for I'm coming home.

Anonymous text: *Such a freak, can't even hold a normal conversation.*

Andrei Chikatilo—Butcher of Rostov, Red Ripper, Rostov Ripper; Russian. Sexually assaulted, killed, and mutilated at least 52 (claimed 56+) women and children, 1978–90. "When I used my knife, it brought psychological relief. I know I have to be destroyed. I was a mistake of nature." (I could use some psychological relief.) Captured in 1990, executed by single shot behind right ear, 1994, Valentine's Day.

LARRY

For several months now, I have been following her at night as she cruises the bars. Sometimes I think she knows I'm following her. If she walks, I walk. If she gets Uber, I drive. In fact, one of our major problems in our marriage was her restlessness and going out.

Tonight I met her at Curley's. I told her on the phone I wanted to talk to her.

"Okay, not long," she says, "I'm supposed to meet someone."

Once there, I move her along to a table in the back. Soon a waitress comes over and takes our order. The dark paneling and the dark red wallpaper hide us from the rest of the crowd that's there.

"Why do you follow me?" she asks angrily. "I know you're following me. I'm not blind."

"Because I want our kids to have a mother," I say.

"Bullshit, you just want to see who I'm fucking."

"Maybe, I don't know. There are a lot of weirdos out there. A lot of dopers come in from Syracuse."

"Look, I know how to take care of myself. I got a gun at home."

"I worry about you on the streets late at night. Also, I want you to know that I saw Jimmy Watkins in prison a few days ago."

"Why?" she asks.

"Because I want to see what his plans are when he comes home."

"Is he coming back here?"

"Yes. He had a few choice words for you. Can you tell me what happened in school that day?"

She drinks her vodka and tonic with gusto.

"Larry, look, I do appreciate your looking after me, but I don't need it. I was helping Mrs. Higgins after school with cleaning up from our science projects. She told me she had to go down to the office and for me not to leave the room. I really liked her because she was always so kind."

She orders another drink. I worry, with the way she drinks. Drinking and slurring her words now, she says, "Before I knew it, Jimmy was in the room and was telling me he just saw Mrs. Higgins and she wanted us to go down to Junior's office and get a couple of trash cans. He was the janitor and seemed to have been working at the school for years. He had a huge potbelly and bloodshot eyes that never looked open. They said he would get drunk every day on quarts of beer. He always wore gray-striped overalls like someone working on a train. I didn't know what to do, but Jimmy seemed so sincere that I went with him down to Junior's office, which was next to the boiler room. I really didn't worry about Jimmy because he always seemed so shy. He gently bumped me as we hurriedly went down the stairs. When we got there, I could see Junior drinking from a bottle of beer. I also saw a small cot near his desk. It was filthy. I asked for the trash cans and he said he would go get them. He pointed to the cot and told us to sit and wait. I began to get a little nervous, but what could Jimmy do to me?"

"When Junior came back with the trash cans he said, 'Jimmy, you got to do it now. Push her down.' Strongly, he pushed me back on the cot. 'Come on. Get on her.' I tried to push him back, but he was too strong. He stabbed me with something and my right arm started to bleed. Suddenly I felt blood starting to go down my arm . . . then . . . in between my legs it wasn't Jimmy . . . it was Junior . . . I think. He was pushing hard . . . Larry, I can't, I can't, please. I can't go on . . . All I know, next I was in an ambulance with Mrs.

Higgins and soon my parents were in the ER. Then I was on the stand repeating all of this shit again and they sentenced Jimmy for twenty years at Elmira and Auburn. I don't know why I never said anything about Junior. Sometimes I'm totally confused and I don't know what really happened."

I move my chair over to her and begin holding her tightly as she sobs unbearably. "I'll make sure he'll never touch you again. At least Junior is dead now. Jimmy is our problem now."

Still crying, she gets up quickly, goes to the bar, and immediately moves on to a muscled punk. She's unreal.

JEANIE

I gave Bo-Jean a hug. She looks tired and worn out. Her clothes are crumbled and her breath stinks of stale wine.

She sits in a chair opposite me.

"So, Bo-Jean, what would you like to talk about? Start anywhere," I say.

"Look, Jeanie, I really need your help," she says. "I'm over my head in my life with the kids, my mother, and the men in my life. I really feel I have problems with drinking too much wine. I know that hurt my marriages, and now it's hurting me in my job at the printing company. I sometimes can't remember things. I think I'm starting to black out, and I can't remember where I've been at times. Sometimes I feel like I'm getting like my mother. I'm just fucked up. I almost have given up on everything and everybody. I have allowed the dark to enter me. My spiritual side has taken a slam. Also, I think I can't afford where we are living."

"What do you mean?" I ask.

"I mean, Larry has been giving me enough child support, but I still have problems with bills. And I know on a cop's salary he can't give me any more. And whatever my father left us is almost gone because my mother gets the rest. I'd just like to make enough to pay my bills off and maybe find another place to live. I'm tired of worrying about Roberta and Stella. I know they get bullied a lot in school and they don't tell me. I'm tired of not sleeping too . . . I'm tired of the heartache I've had with guys . . . I'm just tired of almost everything . . . You know what I mean?"

"Yes," I say. "You want some order in your life and you're

tired of just life in general."

"That's it," she says. "I just want someone to love me and take care of me and the kids," she says. "I'm lonely, even though I have all these people around."

"I'd like you to attend my Tuesday evening group meetings with some of my other clients," I say, "who are having problems with addictions like food, drugs, alcohol. I think that would help. Everyone talks freely and they support each other."

"Okay, I'll see," she says.

"Perhaps we can grab a cup of coffee some time," I say. "I'd really like to be your friend."

"Okay," she says, "I really would like that."

After she leaves, I begin to write in her file, but suddenly I stop. I think I would like to go out bar hopping with Bo-Jean sometime. I had three marriages, and they all failed. My life with Monte is okay but I want something more. Perhaps I'm a little like Bo-Jean. I was stuck in a tidy suburb of Syracuse before we moved here because of Monte's work with the power plant. I was bored. I gorged myself on drinking and had many extramarital affairs. I even had affairs with some of my clients' husbands who came in with their wives for help. I probably caused a few divorces. I like getting in my patients' lives. Some of the guys Bo-Jean talks about seem like the kind I would like, especially the rough sex kind of guys. I know I'm better looking than Bo-Jean. She's getting fat, whereas I always had a fashion model type frame with big breasts. Everyone tells me I look like Jennifer Aniston. Long legs and beautiful, flowing, sandy blonde hair. I also know even though her kids have problems, I could give them the love they need so badly. None of my marriages produced any kids. I just have urges I can't control when I see my patients' lives messed up.

They have drama and intensity in their lives, and I have nothing.

Roberta

I think I will stay up tonight until she comes home. Anna went to bed early. I need to tell my mom what's going on in my life. She should be home soon. It is one in the morning. Maybe I'll give her the letter.

At three thirty, I hear her come in the front door. I was asleep on the sofa. The TV is on with old Westerns.

"Mom, are you okay?" I ask as she looks surprised to see me getting up from the sofa and going over to her. I am shocked to see her clothes and a face that looks bruised and bloody.

"Mom, what the hell happened to you?" I ask, worriedly.

"Nothing," she says, touching her face now. "I fell getting into the car, I think."

"Look, let me get a washcloth." I go get a wet washcloth. I then move her over to the sofa, and she sits.

I begin to wash off the dried blood caked on the right side of her face. Her clothes are wrinkled and messy.

"Maybe, Mom, we should go to the ER," I say.

"No, I'm fine," she says, slurring her words.

"Mom, you got to stop this going out."

"I know," she says, sobering up fast. "I blacked out, I think. It scares me."

For a moment, neither of us move. Then I pull her close to me. "Mom, I love you. You really got to stop this."

"I love you, too," she says. "Don't worry. I'll be okay. But why are you up?"

"I wanted to talk to you about something, but I don't know now."

"What is it, honey? Look, I'm okay. Don't worry," she says. "I'm working on getting better. Jeanie's helping. Anyway, tell me what's going on?"

"Mom, I don't like being a girl anymore," I say, holding my breath that she'll be mad.

She put her arms around me and says, "Baby, that's okay. Sometimes I wish I wasn't a woman, too. But just be yourself. Once I get myself straight, we'll take a long vacation with Stella. Okay?"

"Okay. I love you, Mom."

"And I love you in whatever you want to be."

I decided not to give her the letter, but it was all out now, and I felt tremendous relief.

ANNA

Today, I think I will get some stew meat from Rossi's on Wall Street. I haven't driven in a long time. I remember how Fred would love to go for rides on Sundays. We loved the rural roads and finding farms or stores on our travels. Bo-Jean used to come with us and wanted to always move because she would say, at even seven years old, she loved the peace and quiet. Fred and I would dream about having a farm with horses, cows, and other animals. But because of his business he needed to be near a city like Syracuse.

Before he died, he bought a new Caddy. He always said if he was in an accident he wanted to be safe in a big car. I haven't been in the car since I got out of that awful place where they treated me like I was some crazy person.

Anyway, the Caddy starts right up as I drive to Wall Street. Bo-Jean keeps the Caddy in her two-door garage and tells me she started it every so often when I was gone to Oakdale.

I head on toward Wall Street where I think Rossi's is, but I must have taken a wrong turn because I am now on Route 20 heading to Rochester. So, I think Fred and I have been there several times, but I am now on Route 251, and I turn on Route 864 and perhaps that will bring me to Rochester. Now, I am in a place called Interlochen. It is getting dark, and I think, God, Fred, and I were on these roads every Sunday, but now I am parked in a parking lot of the American Winery. What should I do? Fred, help me. I look for my cell phone, but I can't find it in my purse. There are not enough good signs in New York rural areas. They take care of the cities like Syracuse and Rochester but not small towns. I travel down the road and see now that I am in Ithaca. I pull into another parking lot of a shopping center and just think I will just sit here for a while until my head gets cleared. It is buzzing and hurting now. "Mommy, I'm lost," I say out loud. She'll come find me. She always does. "I'm scared thinking I will never find home again. The monster will come and eat me."

Bo-Jean

It's five o'clock in the afternoon and where the hell is my mother? I saw that the Caddy is missing. I want her to watch the girls. I have to get out tonight. I'm terribly hungry. I fed the kids some left-over spaghetti and meatballs. They both seem in their own worlds tonight. They eat a little and quickly go back to their rooms and computers. I drink almost a half of a bottle of wine. Where the fuck are you, Mom? That's all I need, I think, is for her to be in an accident. I never think perhaps she can't drive anymore.

Finally, at about nine o'clock, I get a call from the security police at the Ithaca Mall. They found my mother disoriented and confused in her car. They found my name and phone number on the back of an old birthday card she had in her purse. They are going to bring her into the mall security office and wait until I can come and get her.

"Shit, shit," I scream as I hang up. That's about an hour and a half away. Still, I can go out about midnight when I get back.

I call Larry and ask him if he will send one of his people to pick up the car keys tomorrow. I will leave the keys with security at the Ithaca Mall. He also wants to know if I want him to come along with me.

"No, thank you. I just got to deal with her and what is happening to her mind. Just check on the kids later."

"Okay, I'm here if you need me to go along," he says.

"Thanks," I say as I hang up and begin my journey to Ithaca. I know what my problem is, and Larry can't take care of that need. I am horny and need to get laid. I want somebody and I don't want to get involved. I often think, after what Jimmy and Junior did to me I hated doing it on the one hand, but on the other I needed it.

Later, as I am driving back with my mother I ask, "Mom, what happened? You were going to pick up some meat at Rossi's you said. I should have told you he and his son went out of business when you were in Oakdale."

"Well, I don't know," she says, "I looked and looked and then I thought I would take a ride like your father and me used to do. I don't know what happened."

"Mom, I don't want you to take the car out alone anymore. Okay?"

"I'll see, I won't get lost again," she says stubbornly.

Perhaps I should have stayed married to Larry, but I just couldn't stay faithful to him. That's always been my problem. When I get home, I make sure my mother is doing okay before I leave. She immediately begins watching *The Tonight Show* with Jimmy Fallon. I check on the kids. They are both in their beds. Then I change into a black jersey skirt and a tight black turtle-neck, which makes my breasts seem full like when I was pregnant.

They kept asking me if he hurt me. All I remember is something stabbing my arm. I was crying uncontrollably. My eyes were tightly closed.

"You're not doing anything, Jimmy." Junior violently pushed Jimmy off me as he got on me. I still can smell his stale beer breath. My pants were off now as I felt something inside of me as I went numb. I wanted to throw up, and I think I did, swallowing the vomit. Nothing was the same since then. The pain was part of it, but it went deeper than that. Loneliness came and never left me.

"Stop!" I heard myself scream. "No more." My stomach hurt. I was still crying hard, so hard I couldn't catch my breath and the

next thing I remember someone hit my face with his fist. Every-thing went black then.

KAY

"I'm coming in tomorrow night with a friend who I think you'll like," I say.

"Will you be staying over?"

"No. I have to go on to Rochester for a big fashion show. Look, I've told him all about you. That you're the most beautiful person I know."

"You're such a bullshitter," Bo-Jean says.

"Hey, just go out with him tomorrow night. If you don't like him, dump him, okay?"

"Shit. I don't know."

"Please. What do you have to lose? Look, he's staying at the Holiday Inn in Auburn. Meet us at around six at the Holiday Inn's Wagon Wheel. I have to be in Rochester at eight. And please wear something sexy—no sweatshirt."

"Okay. I'll wear the latest from Prada," Bo-Jean laughs.

"Asshole," I say kiddingly.

Bo-Jean

It took me a while to get Mom to understand what is going on. Ever since I took the car keys away from her, she's been pissed at me, but I think the getting lost really scared her.

Driving over to Auburn, I think, why am I doing this? Damn Kay. Last weekend I also met this guy Oliver Fisher at the Wagon Wheel. This is almost twice in one week. He was in town working with some people who wanted to put in a huge casino in the central New York area. He is a corporate lawyer who works for the State of New York. The kids were with Larry for the weekend, so I was free from Friday to Sunday. I met him at the bar.

"You come here much?" he asked.

"Sometimes," I said.

"You live around here?" he asked.

"I guess," I said.

This small talk is such bullshit, but it's all part of the game for sex.

"Hey, I understand you being so evasive," he said. "I might be a serial killer."

I laughed a little, but he's right: you never know who you're going to meet at a bar. That's what Larry has been trying to tell me for months. "I live nearby in Port Byron. And I have two kids who live in two worlds. I'm also losing my mom to the other world."

"I know what you mean," he said. "I just lost my mom at eighty-five. She became a blank slate with Alzheimer's."

"She's not blank yet," I said. "But sometimes I wonder."

"Yeah. I know."

I just don't know about him. He was sort of a big guy with a red beard. He seemed to be one of these teddy bear types.

"I see by your ring that you're married. How many kids do you have?"

"Two," he said. "Jane is twelve and my boy, Jeffrey, is fifteen."

"That's nice." I really didn't care, but I guess when in a bar everything is dark, and if you have a few drinks, there is a certain closeness you form with others at the bar.

He smiled. "I've been married for almost eighteen years."

He doesn't look that old. At most, he looked mid-thirties.

"Look, you wanna get out of here?" he asked.

"Sure," I said. "I just stopped in for just one drink." I lied because I needed to take care of my need. "Okay," I said. "Hey, what is your name anyway?"

"Oliver Fisher," he answered. "What's your name?"

"Bo-Jean Franklin," I said.

"Are you a hillbilly?"

"Nope. I'm originally from here. My mom just loved country singers."

"I love it," he said, laughing.

"Let's walk for a while," I said. "I need to work off some of my energy."

"That's fine," he said.

We began to walk away from the hotel toward the downtown area of Auburn. I liked walking with him because he was big and I felt comfortable. There weren't many people in the downtown area. In fact, like many small towns in America, there are hardly any stores left except for small boutiques and coffee shops. Walmart has killed them off, one by one.

"Are you happily married?" I asked.

"No, but I'm staying until the kids go off to college," he said.

"I can't see how you could live that way, you know what I mean?" I asked.

"It's not easy," he said. "But I love my kids and Lisa is a good woman," he said.

"She must be," I said.

"Right now that's how I'm willing to live. You don't think I'm crazy?" he asked.

"No, I understand."

At a diner called Hunter's we turned and headed back to the hotel. He went on to tell me how when he goes away on business, ultimately he looks for bars so he can take care of what he doesn't get at home. Not so much for sex but for companionship. He sort of also has a steady girl who is a neighbor. Her name is Shirley, and they do a lot of pot together, which he said, that along with sex and wine, helps.

I was getting tired, but he was like a talking machine now, but it was okay. I enjoyed talking to him, and it took my mind off my life of going nowhere. I'm so alone. Then he went on to tell me his girlfriend Shirley was a beauty. He said she had golden hair and deep blue eyes, whereas his wife had gotten old-looking—with deep wrinkles and putting on the pounds. He also said the first time he met Shirley she sent a sexual shiver throughout his body like getting an electrical shock treatment.

"My wife wanted me to drop off a Christmas gift to her. She was a neighbor. Anyway, that's how it all got started. Out of nowhere, that night I kissed her hard on the lips. Soon after, our bodies were pressing into each other as our tongues twisted crazily around." He kept going on and on about their sex together, and I was getting hot and wanted it.

He then said, "I also found out Shirley was like me and was an ex-Catholic and was fed up with its dogma about divorce, gays, and abortion. In short, we hated the oppressive nature of the Church. We both sought something more spiritual and had both found it in the readings of Edgar Cayce. We liked his ideas about heaven. There is no hell, purgatory, and limbo. Everyone starts off in heaven, Cayce said, and comes to earth for spiritual growth and enlightenment. Even Hitler-like people go to heaven and come back through reincarnation to serve others. Each time, on their journey back to earth, undivided, they transform to a higher level of goodness."

"Sounds good to me," I said. I was really getting tired of his talking. We were now in the lobby of the Holiday Inn. He motioned for us to sit for a while. Shit, I thought, enough is enough.

"Here's the thing I want to tell you. We would drink some wine and smoke a little pot and then she opened a portal to a new world for me. Shirley said she was home with her father who was an Indian chief. After a few times I was able to see what she was seeing. Beautiful mountains and deep blue skies. She said because of my tender lovemaking she was able to stay home longer than ever before. She said we were in the fourth dimension. I don't know if we were, but she's helping me get through a marriage I don't want to be in."

Finally we got up and went to his room. It smelled of Old Spice and Lysol.

He asked, "Do you want a glass of wine?"

"Okay, but I can't stay long," I said. "I'm really tired."

He put his arm around me as he gave me a glass of wine and sat on the edge of the bed. I handed my glass of wine back to him as I took off my coat and shoes and threw them to the other side of the bed. He handed the glass of wine back to me as he took out a golden cigarette case and took out two joints. He lit both and handed me one. I really didn't want one, but I went ahead and inhaled deeply. It helped to relax me. I drank some more wine and inhaled again. I was feeling good and relaxed. Now I started to wonder if he was going to make his first move or was he all talked out. Right now I really didn't care and, I thought, except for that time, I don't think I ever rejected any guys unless I could see they were into violent sex, which I didn't mind sometimes if the love-making afterwards was good.

"Did I talk too much?" he asked.

"No, I really enjoyed hearing about moving into another portal or whatever," I said, as I dragged on the joint again.

I leaned against the pillows, dragging on the joint again. He now stretched out next to me and also smoked his joint. He then lightly kissed me on my lips.

"I like that," I said.

He got up, took my joint, went to the bathroom and threw them in the commode. He came back and gently rubbed his hand over my breasts. I was now dancing in the moonlight with Oliver Fisher. He and I were getting married and now flying over Paris. He sang beautiful songs to me. I felt him now lifting my sweater. He was very gentle. I felt safe with him. I now felt him in me, and he came quickly. I also came as he kissed me and then I drifted into a deep sleep. When I woke and saw it was four in the morning, I thought, *I got to get up and check on Mom.* At least I didn't have to worry about the kids because Larry had them this weekend. I patted his side of the bed and he was gone. Every trace of him was gone. Suitcase and all. Everyone, I thought, likes to leave me.

The next night it's the Holiday Inn again. As I walk in wearing my overused sexy black cocktail dress, I see Kay waving from the back of the Wagon Wheel with its wagon wheels, spurs, and pictures of cowboys on the walls. I can see now that Kay looks gorgeous in a tight black leather suit. Her silky, sandy brown hair sits perfectly on her shoulders. She kisses me on the lips when I get to the table. She is showing just enough cleavage to tempt any guy around. Her breasts are perfect. She introduces me to Brad Atkins, a corporate lawyer who works with her when he represents Russ. *Not another corporate lawyer.* He is tall, blond, and good looking. He wears wire-rimmed glasses, and I think perhaps he is a surfer and has probably screwed every woman he has met. I am really not in the mood for him, especially after last night.

We order our drinks as Kay begins.

"Brad has been working on getting us set up with a corporate office in Syracuse. So I told him to stay here in Auburn and meet my friend."

"So, Brad, how many years have you been with Russ?" I ask.

"Six," he says. "I tried working for a firm on Wall Street for a while. But it got boring. Anyway, Bo-Jean, why don't you tell me what you do?"

"Hang around bars," I say. "And I try to pick up guys . . ." Smartass.

Kay interrupts, "She doesn't. She worked with me at Russ for a few years. She's got a master's in literature from Yale. And now she works in PR for a printing company."

"Only part time," I say. "I got two kids and a mother I also have to watch over."

"You can see she's really busy," Kay says. She touches Brad's hand. He smiles. I wonder why Kay wanted to push him off on me. It was always that way in New York. Every time we double dated, they all were trying to make a play for Kay.

"Are you married?" he asks. He now touches Kay's arm and leans closer to her. I don't know why I'm here. I feel like a third party.

"I was, but I decided after two failed marriages I'm done."

"She had it made in New York, but she met this New York cop and that was it," she says. "Moved to Port-fucking-Byron, had two kids and another brief fling at marriage. Isn't that about it, Bo-Jean?"

"Right," I say. I really wish it was just Kay and me tonight. I want to talk to her about Jeanie and what we talk about. Or how I've been thinking of taking the kids on a long vacation. What I want to do is something drastic. Or take the kids and move to Paris and get a job there. Perhaps work for the Louvre Museum. I just need to discover more about my childhood and how Jimmy Watkins really affected me. I now hear Kay saying something.

"Bo-Jean, Bo-Jean, are you listening?" she says in a pissed off way.

"I'm sorry really. I was thinking about all the things I have to do tomorrow," I lie.

"Well, what I was saying, my dear, is I have to get on my way to Rochester and hope you and Brad have a great time."

"I'll try, but on the way back stop by. I really need to talk to you."

"Sure, hon," she says compassionately. She gets up and leaves.

"Look, Bo-Jean, is this a bad time for you?" he asks.

"No," I say. I finish my drink and order another vodka Collins.

"You seem distracted or pissed off being here," he says.

"No," I say. "I'll be alright." *I just don't know . . . what's wrong.* I know this Brad is a good-looking guy. I mean, he looks like an older Troy Donahue, but I don't feel the need, even with two drinks in me.

"Look, we can do this some other time," he says. "I like you, and Kay was right. You're a good-looking woman and I really would like to get to know you."

"Thanks, Brad," I say. "I really would like to get to know you too." The thought of maybe running into Jimmy Watkins is really bothering me now. The memories of that day are bothering me.

"Look, Brad," I say. "It's not you, because you seem like a nice guy. It's me." I get up.

"Do you have a card?" He hands me his business card.

"No," I say. I take his card and leave. Thoughts of that afternoon with Jimmy and Junior come into my mind. I must get all this shit straight with Jeanie. Something is wrong with me because Brad seems so nice, but I'm just getting tired of myself.

Once I knew Clarence wasn't coming around much, I picked up my cruising and also decided to paint for a while, as my father suggested years ago. So I went to a craft store and bought brushes, canvases, and paints. When the pills and alcohol couldn't help me sleep, I got up and painted. I started with tracing paintings and even tried painting—copying— *The Starry Night* by Van Gogh. I also copied Monet's *The Water-Lily Pond*. I hated trying to paint without tracing representations. I didn't have the patience and concentration. The alcohol was affecting my ability to focus and concentrate. Anyway, I began to enjoy letting the paint guide me. I loved the colors blue, red, and green. The painter Sally Cooper said, "The surface is built, destroyed, and erased again and again, creating a subtle and sensitive history of what has been. A play or dance continues from chaos, a painting evolves." At this time I also started taking Ativan, which Jeanie prescribed. I used to take some pills when I was in New York for my depression. I can't remember their names.

Sometimes when I painted I would become almost one with the painting. My kids loved my abstract painting. Stella said it made her think of the chaos in her life. For some reason I painted for close to a year, and then just like that, I stopped because it became work and not fun. The alcohol was taking over my life, with Ativan as the chaser.

STELLA

Today I'm late because my mother overslept. I wish she would stop going out late at night. She's going to get hurt. On the other hand, I don't mind getting here late because most of the kids are in class, so I won't have too many jerks trying to push me around. I wonder if the bell has rung. I'm upset because the blouse I'm wearing is too tight to my skin.

As I go to my locker to get some books, I notice some girls, Mary Alice, and Beth, and also Charlie, Justin, and some other guys crowding around my locker. *Why aren't they in class*?

They all turned, and I try to quietly open my locker. Mary Alice is the first to notice me.

"Stella, what are you doing?" she laughs.

"Just getting some books for class," I splutter.

Charlie, who is an overweight blob, slams my locker closed. "Look at me, Stella. Look at me," he says angrily, grabbing my shoulders.

I want to kick him in the balls because he is touching me hard and with the blouse already my skin was driving me crazy.

Now Justin chimes in, "Can't you speak, you retard?"

He pushes me against my locker, then grabs my breasts and twists them.

I scream. "Stop it! Please stop it! Please . . ."

Justin then forces himself on me and tries to kiss me while pushing his knees in between my legs. Everyone is laughing really hard and yelling in unison, "Retard, retard, retard . . . !"

The bell rings and they all scatter. I'm crying now, but I think, they won't be laughing once I stick a knife up their asses.

As I sneak into my next class, which was history, everyone seems to be doing a writing exercise. Mrs. Rogers comes up to me and explains that she wants everyone to write what it means to be a slave. As she goes back to her seat, Charlie, who sits beside me, tries to stick his hand down the front of my skirt. Everyone around laughs until Mrs. Rogers tells them to stop.

I finish the exercise in ten minutes. Sometimes I think I don't belong here in this world. I feel like a tourist in a foreign country where it is so hard to make out what people are saying or even expressing with their bodies. I also start to wonder about why Charlie and his friends get a thrill by sending me emails or texts that call me names, like *Asperger's suck dicks and tits because they all are cocksuckers.* Sometimes I don't even know what those things mean, except I know it's not good. Mary Alice once told me why she couldn't ever be my friend—because I was too weird. She and her good friend Betsy have all the guys chasing them, but I also heard they are lesbians. I'm not sure yet what it means to be a lesbian. In fact, I overheard in math class that Mary Alice and Betsy beat up another friend because that friend was telling everyone they were lesbians. I wish I could be part of the group. I want to belong so bad but I also hate belonging.

I start to daydream about going back home after school and beginning to get ready for the big day. I will drive to school tomorrow. I love driving, but Mom doesn't let me drive by myself because she thinks I'll have an Asperger's episode.

Early tomorrow morning I'll go downstairs, take the car keys from the magnetic hook on the refrigerator. All the weapons will be in the backseat. I know at that time in the morning the parking lot will be almost empty. The side entrance to the gym will be open. Then I will move toward the bleachers to get the rest of the stuff. Now I just smile to myself as I look over at Charlie as he's sucking on his lips loudly and scooting his hand toward my legs. He'll be the first to go.

John Odgren, 16, Woburn, Mass. (Why don't we get those good nicknames anymore?) Intellectually-gifted, ASPERGERS! (that's as close as we come to shorthand for our killers—not nearly creative enough), "troubled," violent fantasies. Stabbed and killed random student, 15, in school bathroom.

His lawyer tried to challenge his being tried as adult, saying Mass. law was unconstitutional, but didn't get anywhere with that. Ended up with life in prison.

Roberta

I usually don't like to bother Stella at night because any knock or disturbance sends her into a catatonic state. Tonight, I don't care for I heard what happened in school today.

Slowly I open the door and see her sitting in front of her computer, staring at different guns. I know she and Mom are into that kind of stuff, but it's not for me.

Gently, I tap her on the shoulder. "I'm looking at getting new rifles for me and Mom," she says, turning around facing me. She seems very relaxed tonight.

"That's good," I say. "But that's not why I came in. I heard what Charlie did to you today."

"Yeah, that's okay," she says. "Soon I will take care of him. I have a hate list in my book."

"Well, he's made fun of me, too, and even posted a photo of me on Facebook calling it 'Or he/she.'" I wonder what she means she's going to take care of him.

"What's that mean?" she asks.

"I'll explain later, but first I want you to know he also posted a photo of you sitting on the edge of the woods eating your lunch. He asked everyone to go up and touch you because it drives you nuts."

Stella doesn't hear me.

"Listen, I also want you to know that I'm trans."

"What does that mean?" she asks after a long while, somewhat dumbfounded.

"Well, I was born a girl, but I've always wanted to be a boy," I say.

"You know what I mean?" I ask.

"I think," she says.

"Look, Stella, I always enjoyed wearing Larry's shirts and even his policeman ties. I'm not a princess model and a girl like Mary Alice who thinks I'm queer and so that's why I wear jeans and boys' shirts and keep my hair short. I know you never noticed, but I always like playing with little trucks and toy cars. And I don't know if you knew I was also wearing men's shirts and underpants that I took from Larry before he left."

"Hey," she interrupts, "I don't care what you are. All I know is I've got your back, boy or girl."

I'm so relieved. I throw my arms around Stella, who stiffens and pushes me away.

"I love you, Stel," I say. I turn around and go back to my room, crying and thinking tomorrow I'm going to wear a white shirt and a black bow tie. Perhaps to confuse people even more, I'll wear a pink skirt. Maybe, I thought, when I get older I might like to switch back and forth. I might be the new Jazz Jennings who is a YouTube personality.

BO-JEAN

Yesterday, I got up early and made scrambled eggs, pancakes, and sausage. I wanted to start working on the new me. I'm trying to work through the brain fog of a hangover. I want to start talking to my kids over a meal and not always on the run. Usually Roberta comes down first and grabs a piece of toast and says she's walking to school. Sometimes I know she meets Emma, her friend, on the way. I wonder now what she says to Jeanie about her gender. I sometimes think back, why didn't I notice her wearing baggy clothes and Larry's old shirts and ties. I just thought that was today's style for high school girls. I got to open up more with Jeanie.

As the kids come down the stairs, they look shocked to see me fully alert, standing at the stove and pointing to the chairs for them to sit.

"Mom, I got to get with Emma before school to go over our homework for math," Roberta says.

"I don't care. That can wait. I want to have a normal breakfast and talk," I say.

"Mom, what's going on?" Stella says. "You know how I don't want to change the schedule we've been following for years."

"I know, I know," I say. "But things gotta change for us and also for me."

"Does Grandmother know about this?" Roberta asks.

"No, I'll tell her later on," I say, thinking to myself I really don't think she'll care because half the time she's in la-la land. "So, now, Roberta, how are things going in school?"

"Mom, it's fine," she says.

"Mom, I really have to go," she says. "Look, I told Stel last night about me, and she's fine with it. Yes, we have some bullying things to deal with. But I think we can handle it."

"What do you mean 'bullying things?'" I ask, worried.

"Never mind, Mom." Roberta gets up, comes over, and gives me a peck on the cheek. "I love this breakfast thing, but I gotta go." And she goes out the door before I can stop her.

"Well, what about you, Stel?" I ask. I see her only eating the blue pieces of cereal from the Fruit Loops.

"Mom, I'm fine," she says. "I can't talk now because I gotta think about other things."

"I know, but maybe after school today we can talk," I say.

"Yeah," she says, as she gets up, grabs some Kleenex, and her backpack.

Fuck it, I say to myself as I now head out the door with Stella. I think I love my kids and also my mother. But there's only so many things I can talk to them about. Of course, there is the gender issue with Roberta, and Stella's Asperger's. Then there is Mom, and her memory is almost taking its last breath. I don't know why I can't really open up to Jeanie. She just makes me uncomfortable—the way she looks at me like she wants to make out with me. I know one thing, I got to stop with the guys. Good thing my bedroom is on the first floor. I would hate the girls to meet some of the guys I sometimes bring home. I'm tired of living alone without some person I can love and be loved back. It's really not having anyone to talk to. I'm worried that each month I'm running out of money. The repairman who fixed the air conditioner said we are going to need a new one in a few months. My part-time job with Gold Printing pays shit.

JEANIE

"Look, Bo-Jean, you got to talk about it," I say.

"It will help release some of the demons."

"There were some things left out when I talked to the police and the hospital people at the time."

"That's okay, we want to get everything out," I say. "You know everything you have been carrying in your mind is really the truth. You know what I mean?"

"Yes, I know," she says.

"Well, I think I told you that something happened at the school with Jimmy Watkins."

"Yes."

"Well, he chased me down where the janitor, Junior Washington, hung out. Junior was a drunk and all the kids knew it. He had at little cot where he would lie down in the afternoon. I had heard about it. He would drink a quart of beer every day. You could smell it on his breath, even in the morning. He was a short, little, fat guy who seemed to be a hundred years old. He always wore these gray-striped overalls that you would see pictures of engineers on the trains wear. Anyway, Jimmy had me cornered in Junior's office. He shoved me down on the cot and stabbed me with something in my right arm. I never felt hurt like that. Junior was now laughing crazily and saying 'Okay, Jimmy, save me some. You gotta fuck her. She is such a pretty little thing.' He got serious as he was daring Jimmy to do it. Jimmy was forcing me to turn over because I was on my stomach and holding on to the underside of the cot but Jimmy was too strong and broke my grip on the cot and turned me over and I could see his dark red face and feel his heavy breathing and then I heard him unzipping and then nervously and violently he opened up my blouse and pulled down my panties. I'm so confused, maybe it was Junior. It's all so fuzzy and dark now, but I do remember screaming. 'Please don't! Please don't!' I was choking on my tears as I felt his thing on my stomach. Now Junior was standing over us, holding the bottle of beer. His laughing was like he was choking on it now. 'Get in there,' he yelled. 'What the hell you waiting for? Are you chicken?' I screamed again, 'Don't, don't.' Jimmy pressed his hand over my mouth. I bit it and felt blood in my mouth. He still pressed hard. Junior now yelled, 'Get off her!' I could see his overalls were down around his ankles now. I also could see him pulling Jimmy off and he fell on me as I felt his penis in me as I continued to cry, 'Please don't, don't.' He placed his filthy hands on my mouth. I also bit it hard. He was sticking something flat and wrinkled in me. I smelled stale beer. I open my eyes and see Junior's bulging eyes close and I felt his saliva on my cheeks. Soon after, he got off me to pull up his overalls. I could see Jimmy sitting in a big, spoked office chair, swiveling around and around. Jimmy came over to me and bent down and said, 'If you say anything that I was involved, I'll kill you and your parents.' His eyes were on fire and he looked like the devil. I felt blood leaking down my legs now. Jimmy was gone and then Junior was gone. I then rolled off the cot and crawled toward the door. The blood on my legs was getting warmer. I thought, would he kill my parents? I don't know, but those eyes of Jimmy's were like the pictures of Lucifer's: mean and evil. I tried getting to my knees as I got to the door. Eventually my teacher, Mrs. Higgins, found me and called the ambulance. Everything from there was a blur. There was a trial where Jimmy admitted it but said nothing about Junior doing it and really being the one to penetrate me. Junior died a few years after that happened. I'm glad. I hate him. That monster ruined my life. I'm still scared and think maybe Jimmy told someone and that someone would come back and kill my mother as well as me." Bo-Jean now starts to shake uncontrollably and I hold her. I cancel my other appointments for the day and just stay there with her until late in the night.

Finally, she says, "I need to go." She gets up and leaves, and I wonder where she will go: to a bar or home? I hope she comes to one of the group sessions. She needs that support more than ever. I need her too.

STELLA

It is raining today, so I have to sit for lunch in the top seats of the bleachers. Soon will be the night. I see that fat slob Charlie when I open my locker between classes. He comes over with some of his stupid friends and says, "Hi, fag, some of us are going out tonight, you want to come, faggot, and teach us how to be queer?" He then grabs my arm and twists it until I yell.

"Oh, asshole, you can 'feel pain,' huh? He pushes my head against the locker and laughs with his friends. "Queer. Also, I'm glad you walk with your head down because I don't want you to see when I grab your pussy. You understand, fag?" They continue to laugh on the way down the hall. I will shoot him in his big beer gut and then see him gurgle blood and phlegm. I know they hang out in the cafeteria before school starts. There, I'll take out the 9 mm Hi-Point carbine shotgun. Once loaded, I'll begin shooting Charlie and his friends.

Mary Ann Cotton—the Black Widow; born 10/31/1832, Durham, England. Serial killer. Hanged for killing stepson, but probably also took out 3 of 4 husbands (for the insurance money), 11 of 13 children, and maybe 10 others. Arsenic poison. (Wonder if Nannie Doss knew about her. Sounds like they had the same ideas.) She got a nursery rhyme made after her:

Mary Ann Cotton, she's dead and she's rotten,
Lying in bed with her eyes wide open.
Sing, sing, oh what should I sing?
Mary Ann Cotton, she's tied up with string.
Where, where? Up in the air.
Selling black puddings, a penny a pair.

Mary Ann Cotton, she's dead and forgotten,
Lying in bed with her bones all rotten.
Sing, sing, what can I sing?
Mary Ann Cotton, tied up with string.

Roberta

I am rushing to my drama class with Mr. Curtis. It is really the only class I like. I also had him last year. I think he knows what I'm going through. There are so many different types of personalities in this class. Gays, bisexuals, lesbians, straights, and transgenders. Mr. Curtis doesn't care as long as we treat each other with respect and kindness.

Yesterday I received a text that said, *Hi, queer, you going to wear a baseball hat with your prom gown, sicko.*

The other day there was a photo on Facebook of me dressed in black leather and holding a whip. It said, "If you want to be whipped, call Roberta," and it gave my phone number. "This Queen Goes For It."

I wish I could be an LGBTQ rights activist, but it's not me. I just want to be me, and I don't care where they tell me to go to the bathroom. I don't really want to be Jazz Jennings, the spokesperson for transgender teenagers. Some days when I get texts or videos that make fun of me, I think I want to end all things; however, once I knew it was possible for a girl to be a boy, I've been okay at times. I still at times want to fit in and be a girl. Even though I have Emma as a friend and a Mother that now understands, I get very depressed because I feel completely alone. I know my mom wants to help, but she is out there searching almost nightly for that perfect something. Anyway, Mr. Curtis made me Stage Manager last year for the successful *You're a Good Man, Charlie Brown*. This year he told me I would be stage managing two shows. In his class, I feel worthwhile. I can wear anything I want. I don't have to be girlish and I can wear boys' shirts, ties, Michael Jordan shoelaces. I shop in the boys section of the stores and wear my baseball hat backwards like most of the guys.

Usually I have to take a lot of crap from other girls about using the toilet because I still use the girls' toilet. I don't know, but perhaps I'm "in between." Life should be about being happy.

We have so many talented kids in class. However, I realized when I was very young that I love drama, but I can't act, sing, or dance, but I love being around people in drama. I plan to study it when I go to college. Last night at the Hot Spot some old guy who was ordering wings asked me, "Are you a girl or boy?"

I said, "A boy." And he accepted it as he continued to play poker on the gambling machine.

After class, Emma and I run into Judy and Tanya, another set of beauty queens of the school.

"You guys still taking drama class?" Judy asks.

"Yes," I say.

"Well, Mr. Curtis asked me if I would like the lead role in 'My Fair Lady' next semester because this semester I couldn't take drama. I'm taking so many classes."

"Good, I hope you can join us."

"Look, asshole," she says in a hushed voice, "Don't think I want queers like you guys around." Then she and Tanya shove us against the locker. "Freaks," they both say and move quickly down the hall.

Emma says, "Are you all right?"

"I guess, I just got to get used to not being accepted," I say, holding back tears.

"They're real assholes," Emma says as she gives me a huge hug. "Let's go to rehearsal."

Bo-Jean

I finally go to Jeanie's Tuesday evening, group meeting that I hope will help me understand why I am becoming more depressed. They all sit in folding chairs in a circle in a church basement. They have already started when I interrupt a hawk-nose older man from talking.

Jeanie says, "Joe and everyone, this is Bo-Jean. She'll be joining us."

Everyone together says, "Hi."

I say, "Hi."

"Okay, Joe, sorry. Why don't you finish?" His eyes look haunting and scary. Jeanie looks pretty tonight with a tight purple jersey blouse and black tight jeans. I loved being held by her the other day.

The guy continues, "Anyway, as I said, I started to really drink hard when my mother came to live with me. My wife had died of cancer and my kids were gone. I was hoping to live a quiet life and enjoy myself. Caregiving for my wife took a lot out of me. It was for ten years. Have you ever seen anyone die?" He's looking at me.

"Yes," I hesitate. "My father."

"Well, anyway, here comes my mother at ninety-four to live with me because no one else would take her. She also has an obsessive-compulsive disorder. She is a clean freak. Everything has to be sparkling and dust-free. I still remember foil on all stove and refrigerator handles. The hardwood and linoleum floors were waxed when I was younger so much that when she wasn't around I would practice skating and do twirls in the air like Peggy Fleming.

Seven days a week I serve her breakfast in bed. Her OCD is more severe than ever. On and on it goes, along with cleaning her bedroom twice a day because of her fear of bugs and contamination. When I was younger she was so kind to me. She would take me to movies and Broadway shows. Sometimes I wish she would die." He then starts to cry like a baby. "I hate her but still love her. But that's why I started to drink."

A gray-haired man next to him puts his arms around him as he continues to cry.

I'm stunned and feel terribly awkward here. At the coffee break, I leave.

Right now, I'm stuck. I know I'm capable of doing so much more with my life. I should've stayed in New York. I know I could've eventually worked for the *Times* instead of being a flunky at a printing press and going nowhere. At times I really don't care for whom or for what I'm feeling. My heart is dwindling. I need to go someplace I think where I can absorb more energy. My spiritual side is restless. I want to take the kids and Mom to one of those islands that you see advertised on TV with sandy beaches and beautiful, calm oceans.

I need to do something quickly. Last night I was home, just thinking and drinking. I had taken an Ativan. Everyone seems to be sleeping. I was watching TV but not seeing what the show was. I can't even remember what I was thinking, but I do remember this realization wash over me that if I just did it, if I just killed myself, that everything would be better, that I wouldn't have to suffer anymore. The loneliness was part of all of this. The bad, dark dreams would stop.

Last night in my dream I was running towards a sailboat with huge, black sails. I jumped on the boat, but it wouldn't move. It was like stuck in a gooey-like marsh. Then I felt like I was in a bottomless pit, falling away from the sailboat. As I fell, I could see ribs—steel on the sides of the pit as people were using devices on me over and over again. Suddenly I opened my eyes with bright sunlight coming through the blinds. My body was covered in cold sweat. I could feel the damp sheets all twisted between my feet.

LARRY

I feel completely exhausted from last night's argument with Irene. I sit here in the department at my desk, drinking coffee and trying to remember how many drinks I had before I got drunk.

Again, it was all about Bo-Jean and why she thinks I still love her and about my children coming over twice a month. She doesn't understand why I am so worried about Jimmy Watkins getting out of jail today.

I don't know; maybe I really do still love that crazy bitch, but I know I couldn't live with her again. There is something more about the rape Bo-Jean is not telling me. I pick up the transcript from the file. I can't understand why they have her take the stand at twelve. I pick up the transcript and read, "I don't want you to be nervous, okay, Bo-Jean?"

"Okay."

"You like school?"

"Objection."

"I'm just trying to make her comfortable."

"Yes, I like school."

"What do you like about school?"

"Music class."

"So, Jim Watkins chased you to the janitor's office next to the boiler room?"

"Yes."

"Was Junior Washington involved? Did he do something to you also?"

"No, I don't know."

"Are you sure Junior Washington wasn't involved?"

"I'm not sure. Perhaps."

The jury took an hour and convicted Jimmy and sent him to Elmira and then he was to finish his sentence at Auburn. I know Junior Washington was involved because of what Bo-Jean said. But who cares? Now he's dead. Jimmy is getting home at noon tomorrow. I get up from my desk and tell my secretary I am leaving to check on something. On the way out, I get on my cell phone and call Jimmy's house. No answer. I then call Bo-Jean. No answer. *I've got to find her.*

Bo-Jean

I just want to walk and forget what Jeanie and I just talked about, and today's sunset is beautiful with its red and orange colors blended. I always liked the in-between time of day. Sometimes the colors violet and blue are there, even yellow and brown. It depends what kind of pollution is hanging around too. My dad always said that's why I should've been a painter because of my sensitivity to colors that make my world. I miss my dad. I would love it when Mother was out for the day shopping for antiques. That happened usually on Saturdays, and that meant Dad and I had the whole day to ourselves. I would make him pancakes and sausage. He loved them. Then he and I would take a ride to Owasco Lake and hang out at the park. I would love to sit there with him on one of many park benches around the lake. He would talk about his dream to get out of the business of computers. He had some friends from IBM in Endicott, New York, who were with IBM but wanted to be like him and start up their own companies. Later on during those Saturdays, we went to Ridgedale Stables, and I would ride my favorite horse, Saddie. She was big and had steel gray hair with wide beautiful brown eyes. Sometimes my dad would ride a rusty-colored horse and we would ride around the trails that surrounded the lake. I think those days were some of my best times of my life.

Sometimes we would also walk in the country near Steel Bridge. Sometimes there my dad and I would fish. Even on occasion my mother would come. Everything seemed so fresh, the air, grass, and creek that ran underneath the bridge. I would love watching minnows as they slid over the rocks as smoothly and effortlessly as a runner running over hurdles. But soon after the trial, he had a stroke, and I lost my best friend.

Perhaps because I loved him so much, and lost him, my real need is to be loved. Deep down, I hate to admit it, but I want to be loved. There is always this need, need, and more need for love, intimacy, and now the need to be drunk. When a guy says he wants to be fucked by me, it's now like drinking a glass of wine. It seems I can't get enough of either one. I have an abnormal thirst for men and drink. I have no self will. Men and drink are my tyrants. They've kept me locked behind a mask all these years.

Kay drove me to Olean, New York, through a horrendous rain storm. I don't remember much of the trip. We left near midnight because I wanted to get there and get it over with. Recently, I found out I was three-and-a half months pregnant. That's what I get for having unsafe sex all these years. And right now, I'm slipping away into the deepest parts of my depression. Another child would do me in. So I had no choice except to get an abortion. Kay said her friend Catherine White ran a clinic in Plattsburgh. She was an ex-nun. Kay also mentioned Catherine had a medical degree from Harvard.

The clinic was located in a middle-class area within the city of Plattsburgh. When we arrived, the storm had let up and I could see from the streetlight that the house was a two-story with light-blue siding and white shutters. Inside, the house didn't look like a clinic; the living room and also the other rooms looked like an old I Love Lucy set. Upstairs, there were four rooms. We entered one, and it was a bright, all-white room; in the middle, there was an exam table with stirrups. The procedure took less than half an hour. Afterwards, Catherine and Kay walked me down the stairs.

Catherine looked to be in her mid-fifties, with her long gray hair hanging down to her waist. She had a narrow face with tiny granny

glasses covering her deep, penetrating blue eyes. All she needed to
wear now was a yellow floral-print peasant dress. She then would
be perfect for the 1960s. I could be good friends with her, I thought,
under different circumstances. She gave off an aura of warmth and
spiritual energy. She told me my baby was a girl. In my mind, I
immediately named her Mary Margaret. I always liked that name
because it sounded holy and saintly. She will live forever as a huge
love in my heart.

Just then I get a ping on my cell phone. It is a text from a number I didn't recognize: *Can we meet at Seymour Street School at 6 PM? I'm bringing my sister Stephanie so you don't think anything is wrong. I have found Jesus. I need your forgiveness. Jimmy.*

I texted back: *Be there. I don't know if it's right, but I do believe in forgiveness.*

Perhaps, I think, everything will be forgotten if I can forgive him, and perhaps my need will go away. Jeanie has got me thinking. Hopefully, maybe once I deal with Jimmy, I can start changing my life and move away with the kids and Mom. Maybe even I can go back to school and get a degree in teaching. I think I would love to teach and maybe even farm. Yesterday, while the kids were at school, I cleaned the house, polished the furniture, finished six loads of wash, washed the car, planted some flowers, and just kept busy so I wouldn't have to think. I had to get rid of my thoughts. Last night I thought about there was no heaven or hell. Heaven and hell are in our minds so people live in our memories when they die. There is no place where God sits on a throne. It is all in our thoughts. That's the only thing that is real, more real than action and even truth. People live forever in our thoughts. Ahead of me, I see the road to Weedsport so I turn around and I head back to town and get on Seymour Street toward Seymour Street School.

LARRY

I drove over to Bo-Jean's house, and knocked on the door. I didn't expect the kids there, and I know Bo-Jean sometimes works at home. I knocked even harder and finally Anna opened the door.

"Larry, what can I do for you?"

"Do you know where Bo-Jean is?"

"She said she had an appointment with her therapist, Jeanie."

"Oh, okay. Thanks. You doing okay?"

"For the most part, yes. I just wish Bo-Jean would let me drive again."

"Well, she worries about you, you know."

"I know. Anyway, when she comes home, I'll tell her you were here."

"Thanks."

Getting into the car, I wonder about Anna and how she is really doing. I know each day when I was living there it seemed little by little her existence was being erased from her memory. Anyway, at least today she knew me. I decide to drive over to Genesee Street and see if Jeanie knows where Bo-Jean is. For a while, Bo-Jean and I went to her to see if we could work things out, but it went nowhere. Bo-Jean wanted to be unbounded, and I just wanted some peace. When I get to Jeanie's office. I notice her car in the driveway and another one. Probably a client, I think. I go in and wait until a small woman with a gray-haired pixie cut walks out. She smiles at me and leaves. Finally, Jeanie comes out.

"Larry, what can I do for you?"

"I know Bo-Jean was here today. Do you know where she went after leaving here?"

"No," she said, a bit upset. "She had a good session, but it was difficult." Jeanie always seems coldhearted and stern to me. She is dressed in a gray suit that seemed too tight on her.

"Can you talk to me about what's going on?"

"Larry, you know I can't."

"I know, but I had to ask. Anyway, if she just happens to call please tell her I'm looking for her. Jimmy Watkins is supposed to be home today."

"You think he's got himself together?"

"I don't know, but look, I gotta go."

I turn, open the door, and leave.

Bo-Jean

The twilight is fading with the redness turning gray and then stark blackness as I approach Seymour Street School. The school, after all these years, looks the same with its three-story, red brick, rectangular shape hovering over me, as I approach the steps leading up to the entrance. Every light in every room seems to be on. *Am I stupid doing this? No. I need to do this. Perhaps I should've called Larry.* I hesitate before I open the door and now think of my marriage to Larry.

After I met him at a local NYC bar where singles met, we left and got laid. But I remember with Larry it was different. The sex was good but not great as it was with other guys. He was raised Catholic and thought he was going to be a priest for a while. He could never let himself be completely free in bed because of that Catholic thinking that you should not enjoy sex because it was only for making kids.

However, I loved cuddling in Larry's arms before and after sex. I was comfortable with him, and he knew I wanted to have children with him, and when he told me he was going to accept the chief's position in my hometown of Port Byron, it cemented my relationship with him. Now I knew I was going to miss New York City and my friend Kay. But I was ready to settle down, even though at times the nightmare of Jimmy Watkins shadowed me. We had Roberta and Stella just two years apart. My mother was a tremendous help in taking care of them, especially after I went back to work for Gold Printing. Soon after, I got bored with Larry and began to go out looking for guys to fill my need. Larry and I fought about my nightly escapades. In a small town, the police know everything. One night when I came home he said, "Look, Bo-Jean, I can't live with knowing you're with another guy. Are you going to stop?"

"No," I said coldly.

"Then it's over," he said angrily. The next day he left, and in six months we were divorced, and nine months later I married Clarence Anderson on the rebound. I loved his sex but hated his being away on business all the time and also his need to get drunk and fall asleep right after sex. Soon the sexuality and romance were gone and there was not even a friendship anymore. Anyway, I always felt he had someone in another city he was screwing. That's when I decided I didn't want to ever marry again as long as my need was taken care of.

I remembered what Larry said when I told him I didn't like being owned: "Bo-Jean, I love you," his voice was trembling, "it just hurts to think of you making love to some other guy." I knew what he meant for I saw tears come to his eyes and then mine.

When I open the doors to the school, I hear music being played over the PA system. I hear Nat King Cole sing: *The evening breeze caressed the trees, tenderly. The trembling trees embraced the breeze, tenderly.* *Tenderly* continues to play as I walk to my right and move slowly toward Mrs. Higgins's seventh grade room.

There is a ping, another text from Jimmy: *After what I did I knew I loved you. I feel bad what Junior did to you.*

I reach Mrs. Higgins's room waiting for something to happen. I'm scared, so I turn back and run to the entrance doors, but I can't open them. Someone had placed chains and a padlock on them. "Tenderly" keeps playing on the PA system. I now run and go down the huge hallway that leads to the auditorium. I open the door, and bright lights are shining on the stage. *Where are you, Jimmy?* Where is he? I'm shaking as I stare at the stage. *I want to see you.* I try to text Larry, but I can't. I am shaking too much.

Another ping: *We belong together, Bo-Jean. That's why your life is a mess. I know you want me too.*

I hear footsteps running above me. I don't care if he kills me. For a long time I've been thinking of ending it all. I love Roberta and Stella and my mother. I even love Larry but not in a way he wants me to. I see the grand piano up front near the stage. I remember Mrs. Higgins singing. She studied musical theater in college and would sing to the school the great songs of Broadway. I recall *"Kiss today goodbye, the sweetness and the sorrow. Wish me luck, the same to you, but I can't regret what I did for love . . . Love is never gone as we travel on. Love's what we'll remember . . ."* from *A Chorus Line.* I should've been a Broadway singer even though until now I haven't thought of Broadway songs or my love for it. Perhaps I think I'm getting ready to die. All the things I wanted to do for years are rushing into my head. The thoughts are real. What has my life meant to me or to anyone? I start to approach the stage. I don't hear the footsteps anymore. Then a bright light is on me. A spotlight. Then there is another on Jimmy, walking on stage. He looks the same, except his hair is grayer and his eyes seem wild. It looks like he has been working out in prison. He is bulked up. He is wearing a tight black T-shirt, jeans, and white sneakers. I don't see his sister.

"Where's your sister?" I yell.

"I thought it would be best if I saw you alone. I love you." He quickly jumps off the stage and faces me. "Just answer me one question, Bo-Jean. Do you think it's possible that we can make love the right way?"

"That wasn't love."

"For me, it was," he says. "It was clumsy and rough, but it was real, Bo-Jean. Too bad Junior got it right, and I blew it."

He takes a step closer to me. He is close enough that I can reach out and touch him. I can smell his sweat. I know what he wants, so I turn quickly and run toward the glass doors of the auditorium. I hear Nat King Cole singing, *"I can't forget how two hearts met breathlessly. Your arms opened wide . . ."*

My hands are on the door's handle now, but Jimmy is right in back of me, and he violently grabs me and turns me around.

"I'm sorry for everything I did that day," he says. But now he holds my upper arms tightly. "I can make it up to you, Bo-Jean."

I shove him away with all my strength, but he grabs me again more violently. He takes out a jackknife from his jeans pocket.

"We need to end it all for us at once so we can be together forever," he says, now calmly.

I think maybe he's right. I don't want to live the way I'm living now. He stabs me in the chest, and blood pours out. It hurts and shocks me back to reality. No, I want to live, so I quickly turn, open the auditorium doors, and start running as he chases me, yelling, "I want you, Bo-Jean. Please!" My chest is full of internal pain now.

He catches up to me as blood is all over my blue blouse. *I don't care, take me, God. I have no more strength to fight him. I've been fighting him for years. I want peace. I want no more thoughts. I slump in his arms. I see him bringing the knife to his heart. I twist away as he falls, and I fall on him. My blood is mixed now with his.*

Lying on the floor, I see Larry running towards us, but it's too late. I have my peace . . . He's crying. Medics are jumping out behind him . . .

I hear him say to them, "She's still alive, I think, but I think he's dead. Take care of her first," I see him look down at me. "I love you, Bo-Jean. Don't die. I love you."

We are in the ambulance. Sirens are screaming, and two medics work on me. Larry continues to cry. I feel that I am floating above. Everything is bright like early morning.

I'm not sure. I seem to be in two worlds. The bright world and here where I see the one medic cutting off my bloody blouse. I try to say something, but nothing comes out.

ANNA

I get up and feel that I am in a daze. Everything seems out of whack. It is as if I got drunk last night, but I didn't. I just took a sleeping pill. I was worried because Bo-Jean never came home, and the kids left early for school. I never can think of the one girl's name. She is so sad and sweet. She doesn't like dresses. Sometimes I try going through the alphabet to think of her name and jar my memory. Annie, Betty, Charlotte, Dean, Michael, Nancy . . . No! No! I can't remember the alphabet anymore. It's like the doctor the other day asked me to count backward from ten and I started at twelve, then twelve, then twelve, then twelve, then twelve, twelve, twelve . . . nothing but confusion and more confusion. I need to get a cup of coffee to rid myself of this brain fog, and that seems to be most of the time now. I miss him, but his face is almost gone. I used to love how he would cuddle me at night and then massage my back. What happened to Bo-Jean to cause him to be so upset? All my thoughts seem to run together now. I'm now at the counter, and I look at the coffeemaker. Where does the coffee go in? In the glass part or on top? I put two spoons of coffee in the glass part with hot water. It was always so much easier when we had Sanka coffee. Place a spoonful in the coffee cup and then pour in hot water. My husband loved it. What was his name now? Al, Ben, Charlie, Frank, Oscar, Joe . . . I can't remember the alphabet. Why? God help me . . . Nothing is happening to the coffee. The grains are swirling around in the glass part. I wish she didn't take the car keys. I could go out to the store and buy it. I feel like a prisoner. I must get everything down into a journal before it all goes away. I tried the diary two days ago but the blank writing paper was as blank as my mind. I just wonder why Bo-Jean didn't come home. I go to the bedroom, but I don't recognize where it is until opening and closing three doors. I stare now at the clothes in the chair that Bo-Jean had put out for me. I take off my bathrobe and slip my panties over my one foot, but I can't keep my balance. Now I try fitting the pretty, colored-print dress over my head, but it is almost too tight on me. So I leave it on the floor. I'm tired, so I decide to take a little nap and think what happened to that nice man and his beautiful long fingers massaging me? Why are my panties on one foot and the dress is on the floor?

The doctor at Oakdale said something about my frontal lobe, which is responsible for planning and reasoning and making judgment, eroding. He said the lobe is marbled with lesions. It is so damn humiliating. The other day I peed in the bathtub. I know Bo-Jean worries about me, but she has her own problems. Someone once told me what's happening to me is like going away and never coming back. I notice too when I start to talk the words are there, but they come out slurred and nonsensical. I also remember when I was driving, Bo-Jean in the morning told me to stop at the Post Office and pick up some stamps and then go to the store for milk. On the way home, I had the stamps but could not remember what else I had to do. What will Bo-Jean do when I'm completely gone? *Gone.*

STELLA

I wait in bed until I think I hear my mother come in, but it is only Roberta moving around in the kitchen downstairs. The pipe bombs are set and in the bathrooms so when I push the remote the timers will go off at different times. Still, I don't know about asking Roberta if she wants to be involved because I know she hates the kids in the school as much as I do. I pull my notebook from my backpack and start to read what I wrote yesterday during lunch and study hall:

"Today's student plays the role of a passive receiver until given the cue to give feedback to the transmitter. The teacher who is the transmitter is perceived by the student as the authority figure with devices at his hand that will bring the student back to the norms of the institution. He must constantly manifest behavior that represents the collective consciousness of society. For example, he learns that he must obey rules, that he must respect authority, that competition is good, that teaching is the only way to instruct, that the more schooling you have the better the person you will be, and that the American way of life is the best way of life."

You see, I copied this word for word from a professor from Syracuse U. By the looks of his picture, he looks like a good-looking Italian. He's probably dead now. The book was written in the early seventies. Also, he said: "As a visitor walks through the halls of our schools he may hear the following statements from open classroom doors: 'Turn to page . . . List the eight causes. What is the answer to number ten . . . Pay attention or go down to the principal's office . . . No talking, the class has begun . . . .' The statements are indicative of what's happening in our schools today. If a person were to follow a student for six hours a day, 180 days a year, he would see that the student is spending most of his time just listening or sitting and waiting for something to happen. Usually nothing does happen except the learning of rules for playing the 'good student game,' which consists of meeting schedules and bells, taking good notes, memorizing irrelevant facts, and passing exams. Today's student either learns these rules for the 'good student game' or drops out of school psychologically or physically when he reaches a certain age."

I wonder what the author would think about what I'm planning to do tomorrow morning. I think he was a revolutionist that wanted to bomb schools out of existence. I think I'm like Eric Harris: always ending up copying someone else's ideas. I don't know. Maybe Eric would want to kill me because I have Asperger's. He wanted to kill all retards and fuckups.

"The death of schooling is inevitable. The rich kids and their parents control us. They are the bullies in today's schools. You know while we preach equality, our actions maintain the inequality that exists in today's society. Paradoxically, much of society acts like a filtration device and separates the good from the bad. If one is white and has a name like Smith, Curtis, Wayne, Cooper, Day, etc., and the kid is born into an affluent family, he usually has a better chance of 'making it' in the mainstream culture other than the culturally different who are black, disabled, Chinese, Indian, or poor. Usually these groups are filtered out by the schooling process and those children who have an affluent background have a better chance of surviving in our society."

I place my notebook back into my backpack and decide I'm going to talk to Roberta later when she comes upstairs to see if she wants to rid people who are destroying people like us.

Luis Garavito—The Beast, or "Goofy"(?!); Colombian, born 1957. Serial killer & rapist. Abused as a kid—of course. He confessed to 140 cases of rape, torture, and murder of young boys. He'd dress up and lure the kids away, then torture, rape, and kill them. He kept detailed journals of his crimes, with tally marks, photos and everything—a "little black notebook"? Charged with 172, found guilty of 138, but suspected total more than 400. Sentenced to 1,853 years, but Colombian law limits it to 60 years. May get out soon due to good behavior.

Kay

I am worried. I've been trying to reach Bo-Jean all day. She doesn't respond to text, email, or phone. No one answers the house phone, and I can't get Larry, and I know he doesn't want me to call him at his home. I guess I am going to have to go there today. I'm also worried about Bo-Jean cruising the bars. I wonder if she is still on the antidepressant pills. Here in New York she had a little bit of a nervous breakdown because of the pressure of the job at Russ and a guy named Randy who screwed the shit out of her one night and then beat her up so bad she could hardly talk because of a swollen jaw. She would never let me call the police. Anyway, after about six months, she was okay, especially with the pills she got from the doctor. Those pills really helped with her panic attacks. I guess she had them ever since her dad died. I know she is seeing a therapist now and is taking Ativan.

I remember she once told me she knew she was talented, but she never got a chance to show it at Yale or even at Russ. She always seemed just below ever getting a break. At her printing job all she does, she said, is create flyers and brochures for non-profits. Just once, she said, she would like to get a break so that people could see how talented she is.

To: Bo-Jean

Hey, what the fuck is going on? Not sure you're getting my texts or emails. Getting kind of worried and hoping you're okay. I've been working my ass off but I miss you and the guys. I'm leaving today for Port Byron to see if you're doing okay. Bo, please answer my emails or texts and tell me how you're doing. Love, K.

I get into town at night and go directly to Bo-Jean's house. Anna is asleep on the couch with reruns of "I Love Lucy" on. She has a bathrobe on, but I can see no clothes underneath.

I go upstairs and see Stella and Roberta talking in Roberta's room.

"Everyone okay here?" I say.

Both respond, "We're fine."

"Okay, do you know where your mother is?" I ask, trying to show no concern.

"No, but when she goes out and if she's not home at midnight, she calls one of us. It's still early," Roberta says.

"Okay, I'm going to leave my stuff downstairs and catch up with her."

"Okay," Roberta says.

I close the door because it seems to me they are in a serious discussion about something. Perhaps it is a homework problem. I don't know. I leave the house and go looking for my fucking crazy friend.

STELLA

"Look, I've been planning this for over a year. Do you want to help me? Because I don't care. I'm doing it early tomorrow morning. I can't stand those fuckers anymore."

"But, Stel, let Mom handle those assholes. She raised all sorts of shit with Silverstein about the bullying."

"Look, Silverstein will pretend he'll do something, but he's afraid of the jocks like Marty Glick and his asshole friends."

"I know, but I don't know, Stel, if I could do it. I mean, I'm finally feeling almost comfortable with myself, you know . . ."

"Look, I already set it up. Last night I placed the pipe bombs in the bathroom. They're set to go off at 7:15 AM. My plan is to get there around 6:30 AM. School opens at 6:00 AM."

"Jesus, Stel. What about Mom?"

"What about her? She'll be upset at first but might be better off not having us around. She can better take care of Grandma then."

"So you are not planning to make it out alive?"

"Of course not. I'm planning on ending it."

"Jesus, I don't know. I just don't know if I can kill people."

"Well, I'm doing it if you want to join me, but if not, that's okay, too."

Then suddenly I leave, closing the door behind me. I almost want to hug her, but can't. I say to myself, "I'll be baddest person in the world in just a few hours."

They think I'm weak or a fag. I'll show them. Yesterday as I was walking into the school some jerk shoved me into a group of girls talking and they all yelled, "Get out of here, you freak." It is so embarrassing to be treated like you're worse than dirt. I know when I end it all those assholes are going to ask, maybe I caused her to die? Tomorrow I will welcome them to my "Freak Show."

"Having Asperger's," Jodi Picoult said, "is like the volume of life at full blast all the time." My mother gave me a book she read by her called *House Rules*. Picoult said, "It's like having a permanent hangover (although I admit I have only been drunk once, when I tried Grey Goose straight to see the effect it would have on me and was dismayed to learn that, rather than giggling, like everyone on television who's drunk, I only felt more displaced and disoriented, and the world only got more fuzzy and indistinct.) All those little autistic kids you see smacking their heads against the walls? They're doing it because the rest of the world is so loud it actually hurts, and they're trying to make it all go away."

Tyler Kost, 18, Arizona. (Again, sadly, no affectionate nickname for modern Americans like us.) Arrested for sexually assaulting 10–18 high school girls. Being held without bond. Serial rapist who knocked up a 15-year-old. He'd threaten to shoot girls in the head if they rejected him. Used texting, Facebook, Snapchat, YouTube to befriend girls, then get rough with them on dates. Had his way with them in his room, their rooms, out in public—parks, parking lots, etc.

KAY

Something is so wrong. I know something is wrong.

Before I drove off from Bo-Jean's house I texted: *Where the fuck are you, honey?*

I start to drive toward Port Byron's police station. When I get there, I notice a small, white-brick house with a large black building in the rear. I imagine that was the jail part. When I go in, I see a young boy with sandy hair sitting at a desk. At first I think he is a fourteen-year-old playing police.

I ask, "Do you know where Larry is?"

Shyly he looks up and says, "At the hospital."

"What hospital?"

"Auburn Memorial."

"Do you know why he's there?" I ask, worried.

"I'm not sure. Everyone is at Seymour Street School where something happened."

"What happened?" I ask loudly.

"I don't know. I just know they all left. I'm an intern with the police department. I just answer the phones at night. Sorry."

"So that's it?"

"Sorry. I wish I could help you more."

"Unreal," I say, shaking my head in frustration. I turn around and leave. Once in the car, I ask for directions from the GPS for Auburn Memorial. When I get there I park in the Emergency Room area. Now moving as fast as the fucking stilettos will take me, I stop at the reception desk and ask for Officer Larry. Shit. I forget his last name. Bo-Jean never changed her name to his. I always called her Bo-Jean Franklin. Suddenly, I see Larry down the hall talking to a guy and woman dressed in green surgical gowns. As he sees me, he quickly comes to meet me and then pulls me over to the side of the hall.

"Larry, what the hell is going on?" I ask, now crying.

"I don't know exactly. We're trying to put things together. It's Bo-Jean. She's in serious condition." He then pushes me down the hall until he finds an empty curtained stall.

"Here's what I know," he says quickly but full of emotion. "I came looking for Jimmy Watkins early today. He never got home from prison. I went to Auburn prison, then to Syracuse because I found out he had a girl there. She came every week to visit him, and I guess he was going to marry her. All day and almost half of the night I looked for him. His mother said she had been waiting for him too. He told her on the phone he was going to find Bo-Jean and get her to forgive him because Jesus told him to do that. He was going to meet her, and that's all I had to go on, and eventually I figured it out that he probably conned her and wanted her where the rape happened. She's been in surgery since five."

"Should we tell the kids?"

"No," he says sternly. "We need to see if she's going to make it. Right now she's in critical condition. I want to know more before I talk to them and, of course, Anna."

He hugs me and then leads me to the waiting room. I want to run away, but I can't move once I've sat down.

Bo-Jean

I can see people with green and white uniforms working on me. I feel tubes going down my throat and also in my arms. It doesn't really hurt; it's like someone pinching me. I hear voices, like someone saying "she lost a lot of blood." But for the most part, I feel like I am floating in warm liquid. The voices are going in and out. I still feel very relaxed. I now see Larry, then Kay, and for some reason I'm crying inside, but outside myself I see no movement. I see the worry on Larry's and Kay's faces. I wonder why the kids are not here and where my mother is. I think it's okay that I die if I stay in this relaxed mode. Everything like I thought seems to exist in my memory. I see my dad's smile as he takes me horseback riding. I understand there is no heaven or hell. Regardless how evil people are, they're not being burned. They are right here in my memory if I want to see them. I think about Aunt Rose. Now that I think about her, she's alive in my memory. She and my mother were good friends. She called my mother all the time. They would talk for hours, especially about her husband, Bud, who I think used to beat her. Sometimes I tried to listen in on another phone, but my mother would always say, "Bo-Jean, I got it, hang it up."

Aunt Rose seemed to always have some problem with her knee, stomach, head, or aches. She had a sweet voice, but too sweet, and you always knew she could be mean. She would say hello to me when she came over but never really look at me.

"I hope, Bo-Jean, you don't give your mother any trouble," she would say. "Because if you're bad, then the devil will take over your body."

She scared me when she would drop that sweet voice and glare at me like the bad witch in *The Wizard of Oz*. It's amazing that memory of my aunt is still here in my consciousness. All I have to do is think about something and it will pop up in my mind. So my mind is the other world. This is death. These thoughts, I figured out, will live eternally in me.

Now I see a young-looking doctor moving Larry and Kay away from me. I can hear them. In fact, I can hear everything in the room. The beeping, the alarms, the noises outside, and people being paged. I even hear the toilet running. Someone has to shake it, I thought, to stop it running.

"I think her heart is not strong enough," I hear the doctor say. "I strongly suggest bringing her family here."

"Look, Larry, you stay here. I'll go get Anna and the kids." Kay looks down at her watch. "They will be getting ready for school. They're used to their mother not coming home some nights. It's near seven."

I feel bad. I can see Kay faltering and full of tears. I love her smart outfit of blue blazer, tailored black pants, and a multi-colored blouse. Where I am, I guess I will never have to worry about clothes and wanting to please everyone. My memory, my consciousness, will live on like a holographic-type of universe. We are connected to the energy of the world. All of our memories and consciousnesses are all connected. I will miss Mom, the kids, Kay, and even Larry. I really feel bad that we could never make it work between us because I now can see how much he still loves me. I feel sad now. Tears want to come but nothing. In this world I feel I'm in another dimension, or perhaps I'm in between dimensions. I see Jimmy Watkins far away, and if I want, I could bring his memory closer, but I don't want to. He exists but no longer in my world. I like feeling like a two-year-old again. Everything is good. No bad exists. Everything is perfect with the world. I can only think happy thoughts now.

And I remembered that I had thought by coming back to Port Byron it would help me deal with the day in my life that changed everything. In a way I thought once I dealt with Jimmy I could be inspired to paint and ignite the talent I always had. I remember talking to an artist at Yale. He was having a showing at one of the galleries. He said a painter should begin with a wash of black because all things in nature are dark except when exposed by the light. He also said a painting must trick the eyes into believing it sees that missing dimension, which is depth. The dream-like haze I have been living with was going away now. I felt free here.

STELLA

I see the old-fashioned clock illuminated at 4:30 AM. I don't use digital because I hate buzzing and the red lights blinking. I go to Roberta's room, open the door, and see her sitting on the edge of the bed dressed in all black: T-shirt, slacks, sneakers, and baseball hat.

"Are you coming?" I say.

"Yes, I don't know why, but I think I should be with you, Stel. I really love you."

"Thanks, and thanks also for dressing like I told you."

"Okay."

We go downstairs. I look out and see Mom's car missing. I think she drove it to work yesterday, so I grab the keys to Grandma's Caddy. Roberta helps me place the bags in the backseat. When we get there, I see that the school parking lot is almost empty. I park the car near the woods, and I lay the keys on the floor. Roberta follows. The side entrance to the gym is still open as I move toward the bags underneath the bleachers. Roberta and I grab the bags. We now head toward the library, passing some teachers. None of them seem to care that the two freaks are here early. So we just smile as we pass. I can see more students are coming in and are heading toward their lockers. Soon they will know us, and then the whole world will know us.

Once we get to the library, we set the bags down and open them. I take out a 9 mm Hi-Point 995 carbine and hand it to Roberta. I take off the safety and show her the trigger. I also grab a 9 mm along with a pistol and now tell her don't shoot until I start. I have on a duster with a turtleneck, pants, shoes, and even underwear, all black. I want to look good when they take me away. Then, with no thought I begin shooting at the few students in the library. I shoot the librarians. Some students begin to run, but I shoot them. Roberta is not shooting. She seems paralyzed. I continue to shoot. I yell to one student, "May the Lord bless you." I ask if he believes in God. He says, "Yes."

"Too bad," I say. "The devil is my God." I use a pistol on him.

I run to a classroom next door and tell Roberta to follow. She just stands there like a fixed statue. What the hell is wrong with her? I immediately open the door and shoot the teacher, and all the students that are in there. I notice Roberta outside the glass looking in and crying. She seems now to be in a complete state of shock. I don't care anymore. I just hope I break the record for school killings. I rub the rosary beads on my chest . . . "Hail Mary, full of grace . . . Hail Mary, full of grace." Eric, I'm coming home. I run out of the classroom and to the entrance. I shoot at students who are frozen in front of their lockers. Killing brings its own power as the bodies pile up at my feet.

I keep shooting anyone I see. I don't care if they are on my hate list. The rich bitches and Barbie-like dolls are going down. This is exhilarating. This is a high I've never had. Must be what God feels like. I love it. I now see Mister Piccaro, the fat security guard ahead of me, turning to get out the front door. I shoot the son of a bitch in the back. Coward. I'm slipping on everyone's blood now as I keep shooting anyone I see. Where is Roberta? As I get to the entrance, I turn and see all the dead bodies lying all over. I smile as I place the pistol to my temple and pull the trigger.

Headline in the *Gold Herald* the next day reads: **"Port Byron High School Shooter Kills Herself and 35 and Sets a New Record!"**

Six Months Later

Larry

After the funeral of Bo-Jean and Stella, I decided to divorce Irene. I know now that there was no love between us, just sex. I will always love Bo-Jean, even though I never fully understood her. Additionally, I moved in with Anna. Her Alzheimer's is becoming worse. Today, she forgot how to brush her teeth. Robert pleaded guilty as accomplice to the mass shooting. With good behavior, he will get out in three years. In prison, he has fully psychologically transformed to Robert. It's a minimum security prison near Rochester. Mostly he is with crime bosses and corporate crooks. Thank God, the judge was understanding and compassionate. He could have sent him to Sing Sing, which is full of White Nationalists who would eat him up alive. They hate transgender people, whereas guys he is with now are too narcissistic to care. I see him once a week, and we have really grown as father and son. He hopes to go to college when he gets out. He's already started an online degree program at Syracuse U in ethnic studies. He hopes to help others like him to deal with transgender issues. I love him more as I understand what he has faced throughout his life. For me, I have retired from the Port Byron Police Force and consult with schools on how to prevent or deal with school shootings. Also I hope to humanize the school curriculum. A couple months later, I got a call from Bo-Jean's psychiatrist, Jeanie Castro. She wants to help us as a family.

The following was written by Stella the morning of the shooting, and it guides me in my work with schools:

For several weeks I have not felt nothing except one night when I found my mother crying uncontrollably. I wish I could help her but she's in deep depression. Most of the guys she goes out with are jerks, and I love her and also my father. I think about what Eric Harris once wrote: "My body has gone numb to any feelings that have tried to come to me. . . . Sometimes I write about danger. Sometimes hate and sometimes a mixture of all the feelings. I have been betrayed in every way possible and now I have gone cold. Every feeling is now just a word. I have found deep inside of me a thirst for danger and a wish to test death in every way I can. Everything about me is now made up, created by what I want my mind to think. I wish that everyone I meet I can encourage to show their feelings and to not hold them in like me. For me, not being able to feel or show feeling bothers me because I've created something that I can only destroy by changing the way I think but after trying to change it has been so long that I'd forgotten who I really am. Your brain controls everything and is your worst enemy if you choose to make it so. That's why I hate myself and everyone around me . . . ."

I've enough of this world and I don't like it. Goodbye, Mom, Dad, Anna, and Robert.

I love you all.

Stella.

TO BE CONTINUED

See Something! Hear Something! Say Something!

[From the Dominion Post, *May 2014: Sunday Edition, Ron Iannone]*

In light of the recent stabbings at the Franklin Regional High School in Murrysville, Pa., I wonder how many more young, innocent people have to be killed or wounded before we declare a war on school violence.

Here's a brief report card: Columbine High School – 12 killed, 24 injured; Sandy Hook – 27 killed; West Nickel Mines Amish School – 5 killed, 5 injured.

There are, of course, many more that can be listed. But most importantly, how do we stop the killings?

Some experts say we should outlaw guns, knives and all devices that can be considered a weapon. But can we outlaw sick people from finding a way to kill others and themselves?

Since the recent stabbings, the TV and radio talk shows with the help of clinical psychologists are trying to figure out what motivated the stabber.

Similarly, over the years we have attempted to develop a checklist or a profile for shooters. For the most part, it is difficult to do this.

Standard psychological tests or counseling efforts haven't been successful in predicting those students who commit violent acts.

Some studies point out that bullying or mental illness is the cause. The evidence is still not significant enough to say these are the true causes of school violence.

One thing that we can say for certain: There is no one illness that is common among the perpetrators.

Educators are desperate for answers. So here come the snake-oil salesman selling their cure-all and security plan packages.

On the other hand, Dr. Peter Langman, who wrote *Why Kids Kill: Inside the Minds of School Shooters*, suggests more likely violent students are created by a combination of societal issues and the students' background.

Paul Taylor, in his book *The Next Generation*, points out that fewer marriages, more single-parent homes, living digitally, and sometimes not being affiliated with any established religion have caused the young to undergo a drastic change from the previous generations.

Additionally, every time I see on TV the young, innocent faces of students who have experienced the horror of school violence, I want to say to them everything is going to be OK, we adults will fix it for you.

First, we must have a dialogue in schools today with students leading the way.

Second, and most importantly, do what airports have been doing since 9/11. Set up security and metal detectors.

Transportation Security Administration agents are annoying, but we feel safer on planes now. The days of open and accessible schools are done.

Beside this, perhaps WVU, being a land grant institution, could lead the way with our College of Education bringing the best of our researchers together to focus on school violence for the state and also the nation.

There is a huge need for solid research in this area.

Finally, we need to teach students and all school personnel the age-old adage to: "Stop, Look, and Listen."

We are at war, and our enemies may be sitting on either side of us in the classrooms or walking in the hallways. Everyone must be on alert to report the most bizarre rumors or gossip.

Our school attackers may be sick psychologically, but also they may be the new terrorists of the 21st century.

They are hurting our most vulnerable of institutions, schools.

ACKNOWLEDGMENTS

I would like to thank Destination Press for letting me use ideas from my short stories *The Shooter*; *Going Home*; and *Sandy, My Love*, previously published in *Consequences: Short Stories, Poems, Commentaries*. Finally, I'd like to thank Jenna for the cover, as well as Rae Jean and Andrew of Populore Publishing for their professionalism and support.

About the Author

Ron Iannone has degrees from St. Bonaventure University and University of Rochester as well as having attained his doctorate from Syracuse University, with post-graduate work at Harvard. He has written several educational books, articles, plays, and screenplays. His books are known nationally, especially his book, *School Ain't No Way: Appalachian Consciousness*, which has been re-published. Recently, he has also published *Consequences: Short Stories, Poems, Commentaries* and the novel *A Boston Homecoming*. He is also the founder of West Virginia Public Theatre.

He has received two lifetime achievement awards for his contributions as a writer, educator, poet, and artist, and as an outstanding Italian-American in West Virginia. In 2015 he received the West Virginia University's College of Human Services Hall of Fame award.

www.ingramcontent.com/pod-product-compliance
Lightning Source LLC
Chambersburg PA
CBHW021014180626
46814CB00003B/1276